HERDWICK TALES

DAVID LEWIS POGSON

Copyright © 2020 David Lewis Pogson

All rights reserved

The characters and events portrayed in this book are fictitious. Any similarity to real persons, living or dead, is coincidental and not intended by the author.

No part of this book may be reproduced, or stored in a retrieval system, or transmitted in any form or by any means, electronic, mechanical, photocopying, recording, or otherwise, without express written permission of the publisher.

ISBN-13: 9798680255360

Cover design by: Art Painter
Cover image by James Stevens from Pixabay
Library of Congress Control Number: 2018675309
Printed in the United States of America

This book is dedicated to all those long-suffering Estates Surveyors who toil to provide a service to the public in local government offices throughout the United Kingdom. Long may they thrive!

CONTENTS

Title Page

Copyright

Dedication

Introduction

1: THE FINAL VOTE (2002)	1
2: LOST SHEEP (2005)	17
3: WEAPON OF CHOICE (2007)	24
4: THE FEE GENERATION GAME (2009)	36
5: FASTER THAN A MAN CAN RUN (2011)	46
6: PANNUS MIHI PASSIONIS (2013)	58
7: DUE DILIGENCE (2017/18)	73
8: A MAN OF PROPERTY (2018)	84
9: THE GOLDEN FLEECE (2036)	92
10: A WELL-KNOWN LOCAL CHARACTER (2036)	105
11: CUT TO THE QUICK (2001)	113
12: THE U-TURN (2001)	121
13: ACCOMMODATING NASA (2001)	131
14: BUTTING HEADS (2001)	138

15: PILOT OF THE FELLS (2001)	147
16: SYNERGY AND PIMPLES (2001)	157
17: THE INSURANCE POLICY (2036)	167
18: RIGHT PERSON, RIGHT PLACE, RIGHT TIME (1966)	180
19: THE BANK CLOCK (1971)	193
20: THE KEY TO DEMOCRACY (1973)	208
21: THE RACE FOR INDEPENDENCE (1976)	222
22: THE GREAT SHEPDALE BELL (1979)	236
23: FOR THE GOOD OF THE FLOCK (1989)	250
24: THE FOURTH MUSKETEER (1994)	264
25: SEEKING BURIED TREASURE (1998)	279
26. F & M (2000)	294
NOTE FROM THE AUTHOR	307
Acknowledgement	309
About The Author	311

INTRODUCTION

Herdwick District is a large, attractive rural area in the north west of England. Its main, centrally-placed administrative town is Shepdale with an assortment of smaller market towns and many villages scattered around it. It has fells and valleys and lakes. Its western edge wraps itself around Herdwick Bay in the Irish Sea. The main employment is farming, forestry and tourism and in the summer it fills to bursting point with tourists. In winter the Herdwick sheep outnumber the residents. Perpetually it elects a 'hung' Council with the Liberals being the largest party followed by the Tories plus a handful of Labour and Independent Councillors, meaning that the membership and chairmanship of Committees and Working Groups is shared between the parties.

1: THE FINAL VOTE (2002)

As Selwyn waited for the question he looked around the Council Chamber. It was packed with the Members and Chief Officers of Herdwick District Council. The seats on the Press bench were full from the overspill of the public who could not fit into the Gallery above him. All were waiting to hear what he had to say. He reflected upon the importance of his evidence. Then he looked back at the Chairman, ready to answer.

***

One month earlier Selwyn had attended the last Property Committee meeting before the change to the new Cabinet system introduced under the Local Government Act 2000. He expected it to be lively. That Committee had only one item on its agenda; approval of the terms for the sale of Council-owned grazing land off Sparrow Hawk Lane in Shepdale to Twosheds Housing Association to build 120 affordable homes to rent for local people nominated to the tenancies by the Council. It would be the biggest housing scheme to be built in the district since the Council-estates of the 1950s and certainly the most controversial. The residents of the adjacent Sparrow Hawk Council-housing estate (now mostly privately-owned because of Right to Buy) as well as the owners of the wealthier residences nearby had formed an ill-fitting alliance to frustrate the disposal process at every stage.

The Planning Application submitted by the Housing Association had been a bitter, hard-fought three-year battle before consent was finally granted. Now those residents were pinning their hopes on the recent electoral changes within the Council membership which, although not significantly altering the balance of the hung Council (the Tories being the largest party but without an overall majority) may have brought fresh minds to the decision-making process. The Planning decision could not now be over-turned. However, the original decision in principle by the Property Committee to sell the land subject to planning consent being granted, taken three years ago, could still be reversed or the recently-negotiated terms on which it was to be sold could still be rejected.

***

Selwyn, the Council's Property Manager, was a grizzled veteran of many lengthy property battles and thought, as he neared retirement age, that he'd seen everything that there was to be seen in local government; many things too frequently, which was a sure sign that it was time for him to call it a day. As he'd aged it had become harder to do the job. Once planning consent would have been a quick and simple task; mark an area with a red line on a plan, fill in a foolscap form and seek an outline decision from the Planning Committee. Now it was impossible to obtain outline consent. Instead, the Planners needed full development lay-outs, ground contamination investigations, traffic-impact studies, environmental-impact studies, flood-impact studies, housing-needs surveys and the rest before any application would be considered.

It was the same with the land sale negotiations. No longer could Selwyn just identify the land on a map, stick an advert in the local paper and invite bids from the local builders. Now, special terms had to be inserted to restrict the houses to local people only, to rented housing only, to main residences not second homes, to special mixes and types of houses to meet varying local need, with clawbacks so that the houses could not be sold off for profit by the Housing Association further down the line and with reserved nomination rights so that the Council could decide who was local and who was best qualified amongst those locals to be given the tenancies. Whilst Selwyn was at the height of his experience as a surveyor he was in the depths of his energy levels as an employee; his enthusiasm had started to erode when the emphasis had changed from getting the best deal for the Council to getting the best solution for the community. It was not that he disagreed with the principle of providing affordable homes, it was just that he had seen it all before and seen it done simpler and better in the past; when the Council had built and managed its own Council houses. Now the partnership developments with Housing Associations made the process expensive, overly complex to achieve and remote from democratic accountability once the land was sold.

He had presented his report on the negotiated terms for the sale of the land at Sparrow Hawk Lane to the Property Committee in the Council Chamber. It was a lofty, rectangular room converted from a former Sessions Court within the Victorian Town Hall in Shepdale Town Centre. The room had small, ceiling-level windows (to prevent prisoners escaping from the former Courts) which could not be opened. The Town Hall's ancient central heating system, supplied by a boiler that could have powered the Titanic but which lacked sophisticated temperature controls, made the room stuffy and uncomfortable.

The Committee Chairman, the Council's Solicitor and Jim, the Committee Clerk, sat behind an oak-panelled bench on a raised platform across one end of the room. Below them, at the far end of the room behind a matching bench, sat the local Press representatives. They had strolled in from the main Town Hall corridor with the Members of the Committee who now sat in the central well of the room behind rows of similar fixed benching but facing each other, with their agenda papers resting on the bench surfaces. The public sat above them in a panelled Gallery running along one side of the room, accessed by a staircase leading from the main corridor of the Town Hall. Selwyn could look up and see them above him from his seat behind one of the Members' benches in the central well of the Chamber at the extreme end nearest to the Chairman's platform. The Committee was not well-attended. Jim checked the absentees and confirmed that there was the minimum number present necessary to provide a quorum to make the vote legal under the Council's constitution.

Selwyn noticed that Councillor Cedric Symons had walked to the end of the Members' row opposite him, under the Gallery, and was now sat on his own directly facing him.

Cedric was a pleasant character, rumoured to be almost ninety years old. Recently widowed, he now lived alone outside Shepdale but still looked after himself well. He was small and neat and always wore a suit, shirt and tie to the meetings and, being quiet and dignified and polite, he kept his own company and his own counsel. He had served his local, rural ward for the last forty years as an Independent. Selwyn wondered why Cedric kept turning up to meetings. How did he raise the enthusiasm to want to bother at his age? He thought that Cedric had aged since he had last seen him. It had been noticeable over the last couple of years that Cedric had virtually ceased to contribute in debates and often, with his eyes closed, appeared to be asleep through many of the meetings, sometimes missing the vote although, to be fair, always participating on issues that affected his ward. Cedric pushed his chair back, rested his head and shoulder against the corner panelling behind him, closed his eyes and succumbed to the warmth.

The Chairman opened the meeting, speaking about how important the development would be for those in housing need within the District and then invited Selwyn to summarise his report on the detailed terms. Then the Chairman invited comments from the Members. A newish Liberal stood up to speak. Selwyn guessed that he was one of the recent election's annual intake. The Council elected one third of its members every year for three years with no elections in the fourth year in a rolling process rather than electing the whole Membership every four years.

The new Member received a cheer from the Gallery. He began to review the faults in the planning decision, to rubbish the housing needs evidence and to protest at the negotiated terms. His main arguments were that the houses were not needed, that this was the wrong site, that the impact upon the local roads and schools would be unbearable and that none of the surrounding residents wanted to live next to houses occupied by ex-offenders, drug addicts and off-comers. Further loud cheers followed his main request; that the Committee should refuse to sell the land and so prevent the development. As he sat down spontaneous applause and cheering broke out from the Gallery. A few Members broke with protocol and joined in.

The Chairman called for silence, reminding Members of the standard of behaviour expected of them. Hands went up and the Chairman selected someone that he knew would put the opposite view. That view was not well-received in the Gallery. A pattern was established: applause and cheering for those speaking against the sale and booing and shouting of insults at its supporters.

Herdwick was a large but relatively sparsely-populated rural district with Shepdale, its largest town, set in the centre. Its scenery attracted second-home and holiday-cottage buyers, pricing out the locals and consequently forcing village schools, post offices, surgeries and pubs to close from a lack of all-year round business. Right to Buy sales had decimated the rented Council-housing stock. New affordable rented housing was needed to stop younger people from leaving, to balance against the problems of an ageing population and to keep the services and amenities in use. All parties wanted more affordable housing but whenever a site was selected there was always opposition.

Selwyn despaired of the members. 'They all want affordable housing but not on that site and not on that site and, oh no, definitely not on that site, that site or that site' had been Selwyn's sarcastic summary to Jim at a previous meeting. He found himself wondering how he could find a way to retire early with an enhanced pension like the former Chief Executive had managed to arrange for himself.

Because the Council was 'hung' the balance could be tilted by a few Independents and they were spread across the various Committees. Having no majority party in control made for weak and inconsistent decision-making.

And so it had proved to be in respect of the vote for the Sparrow Hawk Lane land disposal at the Property Committee meeting. The protestors had worked on the Members, either persuading some to stay away from the meeting or influencing the vote of those attending. Jim leaned forward over the front of the platform and took the count on the floor, noting the names for each raised hand. Five in favour of the motion to sell the land on the terms negotiated, six against. Cedric had not voted. The crowd in the Gallery buzzed in anticipation of an upset. The Chairman called the meeting to order.

'As a Member of this Committee I have a vote on the motion.' He paused, 'And I vote in favour. Also, as Chairman, I have a casting vote.' Another pause, 'Which I also vote in favour. Therefore the proposal to sell the land is approved by seven votes against six.'

There was a moment of confused silence and then murmuring before pandemonium broke out in the Gallery as his words sank in – shouting, gesticulating, stamping of feet on the wooden floor. The newish Member threw his agenda papers across the room. He started yelling at the Chairman. His supporters rose with him. The Chairmen shouted that the meeting was closed, retreating through the door behind him, quickly followed by the Solicitor and Jim. The other Members rushed towards the door into the corridor, some to escape before the crowd could descend from the Gallery and others to meet the crowd to bemoan the decision. The Press chased them to catch the quotes. Selwyn followed them out but walked along the corridor in the opposite direction back to his office. The Town Hall Custodian switched off the lights at the exit and quickly locked the doors to prevent anyone returning to the Chamber from the corridor, fearful that some malcontent might wander in there to cause some damage.

***

'The vote has been challenged.'

Chairman of Council was a hard-bitten, experienced politician. Selwyn had been called to his office for a private meeting.

'Jim has taken statements from everyone present at that last Property Committee meeting. All but yours are useless as evidence. The public couldn't see from the Gallery. Those on the top platform as well as the Press bench were too busy checking the raised hands and recording names. The Members were too busy ensuring that they were seen to have voted to notice anything. Besides, all the Members and the public have a vested interest in the outcome so are not reliable witnesses.'

'What do you want from me?'

'Those Members against the motion have claimed that there wasn't a quorum. They say that the decision is invalid because, technically, there were not enough Members present. The

Council's Solicitor advises that we establish the facts and put them to the full Council. You were sat directly opposite Councillor Symons and saw what happened when the vote was taken.'

'You've had my statement. I'm a professional. I'm not prepared to lie.'

'You're not being asked to lie. However it would help the Council enormously to have the original vote upheld. There is a way to achieve that. To have the decision over-turned would be a loss of 120 much-needed houses. It would also cause conflict with our Housing Association partner. They've relied on our in-principle decision from three years ago to sell them the land, spending thousands of pounds in fees for architects etc to obtain planning consent and they may well ask us to compensate them for any act of bad faith. Likely we cannot refuse if we ever want to work with them again. There's also a lot of Housing Association Grant at stake that otherwise won't be spent in the district and some construction jobs and apprenticeships that won't happen. I've read your statement. Your evidence could prevent that.'

'It's the truth.'

'Yes, but it says too much. I'd like you to remove some ... er ... small irrelevances.'

'I've been thinking about early retirement. Isn't

the new Chief Executive looking at a small re-organisation scheme for the Council's Departments?'

'That's certainly something we can discuss.'

'Okay, tell me which bits of my statement are irrelevant.'

***

'Did you see Councillor Symons sit up and open his eyes when the vote was called?'

Selwyn could sense the Chairman mentally willing him to give the right answer.

'Yes.'

The Custodian had locked the Council Chamber immediately after the Property Committee meeting. Cedric's car had stayed on the Council car park all weekend. No-one had reported him missing. When the cleaners had opened the Council Chamber on the following Monday morning he was seated at the end of the bench, leaning against the end panel with his eyes closed and his agenda papers on the benchtop in front of him exactly where he had been when the vote was taken.

'Thank you Selwyn. I'd now like to sum up before asking for a vote. Normally, under delegated powers, the Property Committee's vote to sell the land at Sparrow Hawk Lane would be binding on the Council. However there's been a challenge on the basis that Councillor Symons died before the vote was taken and that technically there was not a quorum, thus making the vote invalid under the constitution. The Pathologist cannot say precisely when Councillor Symons died but confirms that it was of natural causes. The Council's Solicitor advises that the matter must be decided on fact. If Councillor Symons was alive when the vote was called then, regardless of whether he voted or abstained, a quorum was formed. You have all had an opportunity to read the statements of those present. You will see that the only statement of any direct relevance is the one from the Council's Property Manager. You have heard him confirm what he saw. You now know that Councillor Symons was alive at the time of the vote.

I stress that what you are being asked to decide today has nothing to do with the intention to sell the land or the terms upon which it is to be sold. On that matter, regardless of your wish to support or oppose the land sale, you are expected to put all political or personal feelings aside. You're asked to decide upon a matter of democracy and that rests upon a matter of fact. The Property Manager has no personal or financial involvement with the land sale or the housing development. His job was to negotiate the terms of sale on behalf of the Council and that job has now ended. Therefore it is a matter of fact that if the Property Manager says that Councillor Symons was alive when the vote was taken then we have to accept that statement without question.

Accordingly, as Chairman of the Council, I direct you to find that the Property Committee vote was lawful and ask you to confirm that by the usual show of hands.'

***

Selwyn sat in his office with a box of his possessions, a card and some presents on his desk. He could hear the chink of wine glasses and muffled laughter outside his door. The last six months had passed quickly. He had no conscience about the irrelevances that had been deleted from his statement. He'd been a negotiator long enough to know that everything in life was a deal; that not to reveal all his information was not a lie, that the revised version had still been truthful if only a little shorter than his original version. It was for others to use that information and look to their own consciences. The Chairman of Council had certainly used it for his own ends. Besides, Selwyn hadn't wanted to see three years of his work on the land deal end in failure. And what would it have achieved anyway? One side or the other had to lose; whether it was the residents opposed to the development or the people in need of affordable housing, he couldn't please both. The latter seemed to him to be the better cause to support.

In any event, Councillor Symons may well have been alive after the vote. When asked, Selwyn had confirmed Cedric's eyes opening and him sitting up. The momentary grimace on Cedric's face could have been discomfort. The sweat on his forehead, running down his face, could have been from the warm conditions. The arm quickly reaching up inside his suit jacket could have been searching for a pen. Selwyn had not been asked about those small irrelevances. They didn't mean that Cedric had died exactly at that moment. At the time, caught up in the counting of the vote, Selwyn hadn't consciously registered those signs. It was only afterwards, when he'd heard about the body being found, that they had come to mind and he'd realised the possible significance of what he'd seen. Anyway, it wasn't conclusive. Cedric may just have been uncomfortable or feeling poorly. He'd slumped back down to his resting position immediately afterwards. It didn't mean that he wasn't fit to vote at the exact time that the vote was called. Besides … he usually abstained on matters not directly affecting his ward.

Had he been aware, he'd have preferred that Cedric had not been locked in there all that weekend. But there was no point in letting it spoil his early retirement. He raised his glass and offered a silent toast 'to Cedric, wherever you are'.

2: LOST SHEEP (2005)

Bernard had lowered his voice so that no-one at the other tables could hear him.

'It was when I started to contemplate suicide that I realised things had gone too far. It's the loneliness that gets to you. You can put up with the long hours, the hard work, the bad weather, worrying about money. Sheep farming, no matter how much you love it, is no picnic at the best of times but, when you've only got the dog to talk to, it starts to eat away at you. Fortunately I had enough sense to pull back from the edge.'

'So what saved you?'

'Diversification. It sounds silly I know, but it's the truth.'

Selwyn placed his half-empty pint back on its beermat and looked across the table at Bernard. They were sitting in the bay window of the Shearer's Arms with the remains of their meal pushed to one side. The pub was slowly emptying from the lunchtime trade. From their seats they could see along the village main street, busy with tourists enjoying the fine summer weather.

'And this is all since we last met?'

'Yes. Our meetings were part of the good times but they were quite a while ago now.'

Selwyn thought back to their first meeting. It had been many years ago when Bernard's parents had still been alive. He had called at the farm by appointment to discuss the purchase of a parcel of land at the top end of the village. As Property Manager to Herdwick District Council it had been his responsibility to negotiate the terms of acquisition with Bernard's parents. The land was needed to create flood storage capacity in the valley to mitigate against the flooding that occurred in the winters. Then the small beck running through the village would swell beyond its ability to cope and flood water would wash through the Council housing estate at the lower end of the village. Bernard's field was to have its natural basin-shape scoured out to enhance its capacity with a bund to raise its edges to contain the floodwater and a dam and overspill at its downstream end to create a lagoon. A penstock would enable the catchment to be released slowly back into the stream when the rain stopped, thus preventing the surges that caused the flooding lower down the valley.

His elderly parents had authorised Bernard to handle the negotiations and Bernard had appointed a local Land Agent to represent his family's interests. Nevertheless, Selwyn had cause to visit the farm with the Council's Engineer to discuss the detailed terms and practical issues with Bernard as well as his Agent. Sometimes they had met in that same village pub. Negotiations had gone smoothly and, although Bernard was some twenty years younger than Selwyn, they had struck up a friendship which had continued long after the acquisition had been completed. It was one of those friendships that relied upon Selwyn making the effort to cross the district to entice Bernard out for a drink as Bernard was always so tied to the farm.

'I had no idea. You should have called me over for a chat.'

'It wasn't something that I could talk about. Our meetings, listening to your tales of the goings-on in the Council, were a genuine highlight so I didn't want them to descend into counselling sessions for me. So I put a brave face on it and ignored the problem. That's what men do isn't it?'

'I suppose so.'

'You remember after the foot and mouth outbreak. The flock destroyed, the farm quarantined, the wait for compensation with nothing else to do. That was my lowest point. That's when I began to think about ending it. My parents died within a short time of each other.

There was little money coming in, no future except on my own. I had a choice. Change direction or end it all. But what else did I know about except farming? I was born on that farm, my parents and grandparents had farmed it before me. It was a way of life. And, before I ended up on my own, I used to enjoy it. It's in the blood. But in middle age, with no kids to leave it to, you begin to wonder if it's worth it. Then foot and mouth leaves you with nothing else to think about.'

'I remember that time. I was prevented from visiting by the quarantine. That's when I got out of the routine of coming. I'm sorry for that. And then, when it had cleared up, I had my own family situation to deal with. Now that I'm retired I have more time and won't let it happen again. And diversification?'

'With all that time on my hands I began using the computer. I'd bought one after attending that NFU course in that mobile classroom that used to tour around. I could get on the Internet. I stumbled onto diversification. You know - encouraging farmers to develop other arms to their businesses so they didn't just rely upon farming to survive. Plenty tried Bed and Breakfast or opening farm shops selling organic lamb. My nearest neighbour started a Visitor Centre about Herdwicks. Now everybody's at it - making ice cream, growing mushrooms, selling goats cheese, herding llamas ... you name it. Grants and other forms of help were available and I had the money from the land sale to the Council and the foot and mouth compensation to invest.'

'And despite those more obvious choices, you went into this.'

'You now know. That's why you're here on your first visit in god knows how long. I was gobsmacked when your details popped up in the application folder.'

'It's a great name for it ... The Lost Sheep Dating Agency'

'I'd sat down and thought. What do I know most about apart from shepherding? And then it came to me - loneliness. There must be thousands of lonely farmers out there all looking for love. I was one of them. The country's full of them, all too busy to spend time looking for the right partner, too old for clubs, too far away from cities to bother... and where can you meet them around here? And there's always lonely women looking for reliable blokes with their own businesses and all wanting to escape to the countryside.

So I diversified. Someone from the NFU put me in touch with a guy who could write me an algorithm and with his expert help I built a web-site, advertised it in the farming publications and charged for introductions. At first it was local but then it spread. I started organising events for groups of mature singles from the farming community to meet. I became good at it. It snowballed... I expanded it to include other categories of people with interests in rural matters - surveyors, lawyers, agricultural contractors, foresters, etc. It's a wide field ... no pun intended.'

'That's where I came in. Early retirement was fine at first as it meant that I had more time to care for my wife until she died. Later I threw myself into all the DIY projects that I'd been neglecting and then I travelled a bit but soon realised that it was no fun doing everything on my own. My daughter had her own life and didn't need me hanging around apart from occasional babysitting. I saw the dating site on-line, figured that I met the criteria and thought I'd give it a try.'

'I've cut back quite a bit on the farming now. Would you believe that I'm looking into converting some farm buildings to offer themed farm weddings? The fells provide a great setting for that. My accountant seems very happy about it.'

'Another pint?'

'No thanks. I'd better get back. The wife likes me to take a break but it's not fair leaving her on her own for too long ... after all I know what it's like. So, you have the list of matches on-line. Give them a try. A widower like you with a decent pension shouldn't have too much of a problem finding someone suitable. Let me know how you get on.'

3: WEAPON OF CHOICE (2007)

'I need your advice please ... but we haven't had this conversation ... right?' was how she had started their last meeting some 3 months earlier.

Now, at the end of summer she was saying,

'Things have moved on quite significantly, in a surprising direction, and I want to tell you all about it.'

Selwyn leaned back against his chair, took a sip of his wine and smiled at Farah. She was drinking water but that wasn't unusual. She never drank alcohol because of her religion. It was quiet and private in his back garden; the sun was shining and they had all afternoon to talk. She had been a good choice to succeed him as property manager for Herdwick District Council when he'd taken early retirement. She'd become his trainee after leaving university and now in her mid-30s she was a skilled surveyor and manager and he'd recommended her for the promotion when the time had come for him to leave.

'I hope that you'll be pleased with my decision.'

***

Selwyn thought back to that previous meeting. She'd continued that earlier conversation with:

'Remember years ago when you had a similar problem when you were the manager? You disappeared for a week and then the problem was magically resolved. You never said anything about it to anyone. Now I appear to have an almost identical situation.'

'I'm happy to help. I can only tell you what I did then. You'll have to judge what use that you can make of the advice. All the top brass has changed over time so it's not likely that there's anyone left who will remember any of the details of what happened with me.

'So what did you do?'

'It was a few years before I took early retirement. The Council had to make savings on its overheads. Staff salaries were the preferred target. The maintenance budget had been enhanced to deal with the backlog and the minor works programme had actually been increased, so Property Services had more work to handle than in any previous year on record, so I needed all the staff that I could get.

The Estates section was fully staffed. However, in the Building Surveying section, the Senior Building Surveyor had left and another Building Surveyor was working his notice so that section would soon be down to 50% of its staffing levels just as the workload was expanding. Normally by then I'd have been advertising but there was a blanket freeze on recruitment across the whole Council, regardless of need. I couldn't swap Estates Surveyors onto Building Surveying work as it was a different skill-set. So, in a nutshell, I needed to recruit at least one full-time replacement Building Surveyor even to limp along for 12 months.

At that time the Property Group was part of Central Services so there was no Director above me. I answered directly to the Chief Executive. He was not really up to the job. He'd been appointed when the old Chief Executive had been allowed to take early retirement, as they all seem to do in my experience. The Members were bent on ringing the changes, so they asked Human Resources to commission a set of headhunters to identify candidates with fresh ideas from outside the industry. You know the theory - that a manager doesn't need to have any kind of specialist qualification and that anyone with an MBA can manage professionals. It's madness I know, but that was the thinking at the time.

Anyway, that had been when the national economy had been doing well so they only received applications from second rate candidates because, at that time, salaries outside local government were so much better. In short, they ended up picking a guy who, even if I'm being generous, could only be described as the best of a bad bunch. Common sense should have told them that anyone coming from a high salary in industry to a backwater Council in the North West was running away from something rather than bettering himself. He was bound to be a failure.

We soon found out why he was running. In my experience most Chief Executives, especially the Solicitors, were clever and ruthless; that's how they got the top job. This guy wasn't either. He wanted to be everyone's friend and went out of his way to avoid confrontation. So every decision that he made was a fudge.

I don't know why it is but, in my lengthy career, I'd noticed that every time we got a new Chief Executive, the first thing they did was to reorganise the Council structure, whether it needed it or not. It's like they can't leave well alone and have to change things just to be seen to be doing something. Anyway, he'd taken out a few volunteers for redundancy or early retirement. That way he didn't have to face the difficult decision about compulsory redundancies.

But that hadn't produced enough savings and it all came to a head when he had to respond to the Members' call for more reductions to the salary bill as the Government squeeze tightened. He couldn't do another reorganisation or it would look like his first one was a failure. So, again to avoid upsetting anyone, he persuaded the Members that a blanket freeze on recruitment regardless of need – natural wastage as people left and were not replaced - would be the most effective policy. That suited the existing staff and the unions but turned out to be completely insane as it failed to take into account the particular needs of any service group.

The Chief Executive wouldn't listen to me when I raised the problem of staff resources. His answer was that I should prioritise the work, deal only with what was important and let the rest slide. That was all very well for him to say, but it was going to be me that would have to answer to the Councillors for the failure to maintain the properties. Any surveyor will tell you that if you neglect maintenance it only increases the work and stacks up the cost for the future.

He thought that surveyors within the Property Group could be swapped around from Estates to Building Surveying as and when the need arose to meet workload pressures. I needed to get him to make an exception for me and I needed a weapon to use against him: I had to exploit his weakness.

As his policy applied equally across the whole of the Council regardless of circumstances, I couldn't claim discrimination by race, gender or religion, nor disability or harassment. The only option open to me seemed to be health, more particularly, stress. You may want to examine if any of the other options better apply to your particular circumstances.

I knew that the last step of his Council-wide reorganisation was about to be implemented and that involved changes within the Direct Works Department. The volunteers would go as planned so there was more than a possibility of staff with a construction-related background being considered as surplus to requirements. I had to find a way of putting the Chief Executive under enough personal pressure that he might decide to steer one of them into Property Services instead of letting them go. Of course, he wouldn't hear of it.

I'd already put my request to recruit in writing. I'd explained the problems and the risks and laid it on thick – public safety, danger to staff and contractors, closure of public buildings and escalating costs for the future if we didn't carry out the maintenance. Then I followed it up with a memo directly to him but copied to Human Resources and with a printed copy that I took home with me for safe-keeping. That memo would ensure that I had a defence if it all went wrong.

The memo set out the situation, repeated my request, spelt out the risks again and then became much more personal – it was a formal notice of complaint directed at him as my line manager. I pointed out that the situation was having an adverse effect on my health. In effect I was putting forward an allegation of stress caused by his personal failure to provide me with the resources necessary to do my job and thus protect my health. It was a gamble and it required me to put on a convincing act.

He called me to his office for a meeting and I made sure that Human Resources and the Union were represented as I needed witnesses for the record. He was clearly shocked but he didn't want to fall out with me. He'd never had a memo like mine in his entire career. He said he wasn't aware things had got so bad. He asked why I hadn't said anything before now. I kept my answers as short as possible – 'I have told you before'; 'You don't listen' etc. I was arguing that a blanket ban on recruitment regardless of circumstances was discriminatory on health grounds because it couldn't apply equally in practice unless every group had the same number of vacancies.

At the end of the meeting he said that if it was affecting my health then I'd better take some time off and seek some medical help. That was fine by me. I pointed out that my absence would only make things worse for the others, so he should expect them to suffer too. I immediately went home on sick leave. I know it sounds cynical but stress is the new backache – it's easy to fake, very hard to disprove and I was pretty sure that I could convince a doctor that I was suffering from it in a serious way. I didn't feel good about it or proud of myself but it was a necessary means to an end and I had run out of alternatives. He had all the power and all I had was the choice of weapon.

I sat at home for a week and during that time he must have discussed it with the other directors, and Human Resources and the Council's Solicitor and decided that he was in a weak position legally if it all ended up in a tribunal. I knew that he would feel bad about me personally as he wanted to be everybody's friend. In the event, as you know, you were the one that delivered his message to call me back in for another chat. He asked me if it would help if he was to arrange to transfer a surveyor from the Direct Works Department to Property Services. The individual had a building qualification, experience of the ordering system, estimating, supervising of contractors and signing off work. He was a specialist on roadworks so could easily manage our car park repairs, re-linings and resurfacings and manage simpler buildings like the public conveniences and parks structures, until we trained him up for the more complex structures like the swimming pools and the office buildings.

I knew that I wasn't going to get a better offer – there was a limit even to what the Chief Executive could do – but I could limp along with 3 out of 4 staff. Anyway, it worked. However, I don't recommend that you do this, or anything like it, without studying the problem, weighing up the risks and calculating the odds of success. I was fed up with being messed about by a manager who couldn't do his job well but thought that he knew how to do mine better than me. Maybe I was a bit stressed, at least enough to consider desperate measures, but, let's face it, my actions carried the least risk of any option for me. I could sit at home, perfectly justified on sick leave for 6 months on full pay, let him worry about the consequences and come back no worse off whenever I'd played my hand to its limit. After all, if I was ill, any disasters that arose in the meantime would have been his responsibility to explain to the Councillors. He only lasted another 12 months. His next initiative was also a cock-up and a package was arranged to encourage him to move on.

You do have one other option. You can always look for another surveying job and cite the policy in your exit interview. It might help your successor.'

She'd thanked me for my advice and had left looking like I'd given her plenty to think about.

***

'After our last meeting I did everything that you said. I studied the problem, compared our situations and then talked it over with my husband. However, an alternative presented itself that you'd not mentioned and that became the best option for me.'

'Has it worked out?'

'Well it seems to be going according to plan.'

Selwyn took another sip of his wine while she continued.

'You know that Sadiq, my husband, is an IT specialist and works for himself, mostly from home? His business is doing so well that he needs to take on staff. I'm going to work with him. Also, we'd put off having a family when we were younger until we got sorted financially. Well, now I'm pregnant. I didn't know it when I last saw you. So, I can take on his admin, accounts, invoicing and marketing, run his diary and look after the baby from home while he keeps the clients happy. I'm taking the basic maternity leave but I won't be returning afterwards. No-one else knows about it apart from him.'

'Congratulations. I'm really pleased for you. By the way, I know you. You can be a bit too honest for your own good sometimes. Maybe you should ignore my advice about the exit interview. You never know, you might want to work for the Council again when the baby is older. The way things are going nationally with the shortage of Valuers, it wouldn't surprise me if there are regular vacancies again in the future.'

'That's a good point. Anyway, I hope that you don't think that I'm being disloyal by jumping ship. You've done so much for me and my career. You've always promoted public service as a worthwhile occupation to your staff, giving something back to the community, defending the public against grasping free enterprise, getting the best out of the property assets for the public good.'

'Are you crazy? While I still believe in those values, local government has changed beyond all recognition since I came into public service. Loyalty has to work both ways. We've always had lower salaries, no company cars, poorer expenses than the private sector but the reasonable hours and the pension scheme made up for some of it. Now we have constant reorganisations where you have to keep reapplying for your own job, too much work, not enough staff, pay freezes, attacks on expenses and chipping away at the pension scheme. Constant cuts make it almost impossible to do the job and, anyway, the government believes that the private sector can do it better, even though we know that they're wrong. If it doesn't work out, you can come back in the future if you want to, when your family circumstances allow it.'

Selwyn noted the smile of relief on her face. Farah had obviously been concerned about telling him. *'And if she doesn't come back then once again it will be local government's loss. When will they ever learn?'* he thought.

4: THE FEE GENERATION GAME (2009)

The valley was silent apart from the crunch of fresh snow under her boots. January 2009 had started with heavy falls on the fells. As she rounded the bend in the track she saw Selwyn for the first time and burst out laughing. Selwyn held the 5-barred gate open for her. Two long-horned cattle that were grazing on the fresh bales of hay dumped at the side of the track ignored the noise and carried on chewing. The slopes of the Shepdale Horseshoe rose up around them on three sides. Its white blanket was broken only where the weak winter mid-morning sun, hanging just above the horizon to the south of them, created shadows behind the criss-cross of limestone walls that inscribed the fell sides.

'Good morning. Why are you laughing at me?'

'Well, you're certainly dressed for these conditions – boots, thick socks, gloves, waterproof coat and woolly hat - but the leather briefcase – it's just so out-of-place in this setting.'

'I couldn't find my rucksack when I set out this morning.'

'Did you bring those bales of hay up in it?'

'No, the farmer probably brought those up in his Land Rover.'

'Can I ask, what are you doing up here ... with a briefcase?'

'You probably saw Reservoir Cottage when you were further up the valley? I've got a business appointment there. I couldn't drive up the track in the snow so I parked my car at the farm and I'm walking the rest of the way.'

'Yes, I saw some people up there earlier. It's a nice day for a walk. Enjoy the rest of it.'

She passed through the gate, closed it behind her and then paused.

'I know you, don't I? Or at least I think that I recognise you. Hold on a minute please.'

She pulled a mobile phone out of her coat pocket and began prodding and swiping at it.

'You're Selwyn, widower, retired Chartered Surveyor.'

'How do you know that?'

'I came up for a farm-themed family wedding on Saturday, stopped in one of the guest houses and decided to extend my stay for a few days after all the others had gone. Bernard, the farmer, threw in a free trial of his 'Lost Sheep Dating Agency' website and I remember your photo.'

Selwyn began to colour up but there was no way that he could deny it.

'I know Bernard. I bought some land off him for a Council Flood Relief Scheme many years ago, before he diversified into the *romance* business. We became good friends and stayed in touch. He kind of ... forced me ... to register on the website ... in a way... sort of.'

'Tell you what, now that I know that you've been vetted by Bernard, so you're unlikely to be mad, bad or downright dangerous, do please call in for a coffee when you return to collect your car ... if you want to, that is.'

***

Selwyn had taken Jim's phone call with mixed feelings. They'd met up in the Wandering Tup for a regular pint after Selwyn's retirement and Jim had kept him up-to-date with the changes at Herdwick District Council over the last few years since then. Usually he was glad to hear from Jim but this time Jim wanted a favour that was unwelcome.

'Jim, I detest Asset Valuations. They are absolutely mind-numbing and pointless, especially in a small district council. I only used to do them because, as a good manager, it freed up the other Valuers to get on with the important work without the distraction. I guess that Farah continued in the same vein when she replaced me. I'm not sure that I'd want to come back to do any work, not even rent reviews or land sales but at least they serve a useful purpose in generating rent or capital for the Council. Asset Valuations are just a waste of time.'

'Well, you know that Farah has gone on maternity leave and confirmed that she won't be coming back. There's this freeze on recruitment arising from the austerity cuts so the Chief Exec has asked me to stand in for her as temporary Property Manager. What do I know about property? I'm the Senior Committee Clerk. You know what it is, that stupid theory that any manager can manage any group of staff regardless of the professional discipline. Madness I know but I'm stuck with it for now. What are Asset Valuations exactly?'

'They are part of the Government's attempt to make Council's run their services like a commercial business. You know how if you have a large company you have to put the value of all your property assets in the balance sheet. Well, they think that Local Government should do the same. There's a point to it for a private company – the owners need to know what the company is worth and the value of the property assets forms part of that. But, I ask you, when did you ever hear of a Council floating itself on the stock exchange, or fighting a hostile takeover or selling itself off as a profitable business? I mean, I can understand the Council needing to know what its investment properties are worth just in case it wants to borrow against them or sell something off from time-to time, although it could value those on an individual basis as and when that happens, but the value of Town Halls, Public Conveniences, Sports Fields, Cemeteries etc – it's just a waste of time. I wouldn't mind so much if they were all valued to Market Value, which even the public understands. But we have pointless bases for valuation such as 'Market Value in Existing Use' and 'Depreciated Replacement Cost'. Do you actually know what they are? Even Valuers struggle with them because they're so artificial. Now I'm told that they're talking about something called 'Fair Value' whatever that is. And don't get me started on this new 'Componentization' thing. Even if I could be bothered to explain it to you, you wouldn't want to understand it.'

'I take it that you're not a fan then?'

'No I'm not. We had enough real work to do without them. All that happens after we've valued everything each year is that the Director of Finance puts a few lines in the annual accounts and then the valuation reports sit on a shelf ... untouched ... forever.'

'So why doesn't somebody do something to prevent the waste.'

'Nobody can. It's a chain without a weak link. The Director of Finance wants them in the Accounts just so that he can avoid a black mark from the District Auditor. The District Auditor wants them so that he can report to the Civil Servants that the job is being done to CIPFA rules. The Civil Servants want them so they can tell the Government that there are rules in place. The Government wants them so that it can tell the Voters that they have imposed commercial and financial accountancy disciplines into public services to keep costs down and the Voters have no idea that this work actually increases those costs for no real purpose. The only people who can see the truth are Valuers because we know just what complete and utter nonsense it all is. However, the majority of Valuers are in private firms and they just love that work for the fat fees that it generates so they're not going to rock the boat. So the only people who can speak out are Local Authority Valuers and no-one listens to them.

And there's no consistency. Herdwick Council insists on valuing every asset over £10,000. Metros and other big Councils don't bother starting with anything less than £100,000. Why can't they all have the same limits or exclusions? They can't even agree on a small, insignificant detail like if the Valuation Date is 31st March or 1st of April in any year – not that that matters either. It's just a complete waste of my time and your money to do them, especially in a small District Council with limited staff and resources. I had this view when I left and I doubt that anything has changed since then.'

'Unfortunately I'm stuck on the first link of that chain. The Accountants rule the roost. So I was hoping that you might do me a favour. I know what you mean about it being a fee generation game. I sounded out a private firm of Valuers before I bothered you. They wanted £150 per hour for a one-off valuation of a property or something in the region of £70 per hour if I gave them a sizeable number of valuations in a package and then they'd likely give the work to their office cat. I can pay you because I can spend what's already in this year's Property Group budget from the likely saving on Farah's salary for a one-off 'task and finish' contract. But depending upon what hours we might agree upon that's likely to be more in the region of the local government all-in staff rate for a professional of £30 per hour plus expenses. How do you feel about it really ... old mate?'

There was a long pause.

'God help me!' Selwyn breathed out loudly. 'I'll need one of the others to bring me up-to-date with any Asset Valuation rule changes since I retired. Also I'll need adding to the Council's Professional Indemnity Insurance policy. However, I'm not paying out hundreds of pounds just to rejoin the RICS for a few months so you will have to ask one of the other qualified surveyors if he or she will certify my completed valuations. I know that strictly this shouldn't happen but you're in a hole and those are my conditions. What's the deadline – the end of February as usual?'

***

Selwyn removed his boots and knocked them against the doorpost to remove the snow before leaving them in the porch. He hung up his coat and headed for one of the armchairs that she was pointing to near the fireplace. He noticed that she had applied a bit of make-up since their earlier meeting on the fell side. A faint hint of perfume hung in the air. He stretched out his legs and felt the warmth from the log fire penetrating his thick socks. There was the sound of a kettle boiling through the open kitchen door. Two mugs, spoons, milk, sugar, and a plate of biscuits were already resting on a small table between the armchairs. *'She has been busy. She must have been confident that I would come,'* thought Selwyn. *'Wasn't that the way with women ... they always knew what a man would do even before the man did.'*

'Without being too nosy, can I ask what sort of business you had up at Reservoir Cottage? I thought that you were retired'

'I am, but I'm making a temporary come-back. A sort of favour for a mate at the Council. He has staffing problems and asked me to help out. Every year the Council needs an experienced Valuer to value its property assets. So I'm going around inspecting, reporting on and valuing those that require updating this year. Reservoir Cottage is part of the Council's Outdoor Adventure Service. The cottage used to be occupied by people employed to maintain the reservoir and the upper reaches of the River Shep. When it fell out of use, a long time ago in the past, the Council bought it. Now clubs and schools and sports groups and the like can book it as a base for hiking, orienteering, abseiling, mountain biking etc. You may have noticed the new shower block and store extension added since last year. I have to re-value Reservoir Cottage to account for those improvements.'

'But – I'm really curious now - what was in the briefcase?'

'Well ... invited in, chair by the fire, coffee and biscuits. If she laughs at my feeble jokes then things couldn't look more promising,' thought Selwyn.

'Maybe I'll have to tell Jim that there really is some point to Asset Valuations after all.'

'Equipment that I need for any survey – floor plans of the improvements, notepad, pens, tape measure, small binoculars, torch ... sandwich box, thermos flask, dry clothes ... extending aluminium ladder to access the roof-space ... microwave oven, hairdryer, blender, board game.'

'Cuddly toy. Don't forget the cuddly toy.'

'Exactly. That's why I couldn't get the three bales of hay into it to save Bernard driving them up in his Land Rover.'

5: FASTER THAN A MAN CAN RUN (2011)

'You really did get involved with your properties, didn't you? It's good to know that you still have a bit of passion for your old surveying profession even though you've retired from it now.'

'I should forget about them really. It's just that I'm constantly bumping into them. I can't go more than a few miles around here without passing one of them and they trigger so many memories. Are you getting a bit tired of my old stories and my rants about the Council and the Government?'

'Provided you don't keep repeating them endlessly then I think that I can live with them.'

'I'm not sure that I can promise that.'

'Live with them...' That seemed like another subtle hint to Selwyn. *'What was it she'd said the other day ... about wasting quite a bit of time continually driving backwards and forwards to see each other?'* She'd been making little remarks like that recently and now he was starting to pick up on them. He didn't rise to the bait so stuck to his subject.

'Herdwick is a big district - as big as some small counties - but outsiders think that it's just empty fells and valleys and lakes. I admit that in winter the sheep outnumber the residents but, nevertheless, the Council still has a lot of property spread across it. Did you know that there's only one location in the whole of the district that's at least three miles away in any direction from any parcel of Council land or any Council building?

'How do you know that?'

'I worked it out once from studying the Terrier maps in my old office.'

'Where's that location?'

'I'll tell you when I take you there. You'll be surprised.'

They were standing on the promenade at Lantern-o'er-the Bay, leaning on the rails looking down upon the incoming tide lapping against the base of the sea-wall. The sun was shining, with only a faint hint of a breeze and the fells around the edge of the bay stood out prominently against a clear blue sky. To their right was the shell of Lantern Lido, a sad reflection of the past glory of the Edwardian seaside resort. Now its windows were bricked up, its gates locked and its walls covered with the graffiti from some wannabe Banksy.

'You've not told me about that eyesore. What's the Council going to do with it?'

'Well, when I was Property Manager, I advised them to demolish it and clear the site. As soon as I'd said that some local busybody asked the Secretary of State for the Environment to list it as a Building of Special Architectural or Historic Interest. So he did ... and now the Council's stuck with it. They don't have any money to maintain it, never mind restore it, and can't demolish it so it just sits there slowly rotting away. We used to jokingly describe it as 'planned obsolescence' in the office.

'Why would anyone want to keep it?'

'It's the curse of the geriatric generation – nostalgia. The wrinklies outnumber the young people in Lantern and, being well-educated, fairly wealthy and with nothing else to do they have time to interfere for no good purpose. Many of them must have learnt to swim in there after the Second World War. So they think that the Lido must be preserved forever for that reason. Inside those barricaded walls is an unheated, sea-filled open-air swimming pool. Nobody in their right mind would swim in it. Did I ever tell you about my memory of it? My mother brought me here when I was about twelve years old. I stripped off, dived in, climbed out, dried myself and never went near it again. It was the coldest experience of my life. So I don't think that this current crop of obese, centrally-heated, Mario Brothers-playing computer-age kids would thank anyone for restoring it.'

'It seems a bit silly to preserve it when they have a new, warm indoor pool to replace it.'

'You'd think so, but that's closed recently. That's another sad story of wasted public money. A failure of the Big Society initiative.'

'What exactly is the Big Society initiative?'

'Good question. Nobody really knows – not even those who work in Central and Local Government. The Government described it as giving citizens, communities and local government the power and information they need to come together, solve the problems they face and build the Britain they want. Everyone loosely interprets it as allowing community groups to take over the running of public properties.

The new indoor pool could be an example of the Big Society in action. Because the Council would not spend the District's money on restoring the old Lido the residents of Lantern formed a Charitable Community Group. Then they commissioned a study from the local University to justify building a new indoor pool on the basis that it could be run by volunteers at a profit when virtually every other public pool in the country runs at a loss. It was built with over a £1million of Lottery Grant on a site leased for a nominal rental from the Council by the Community Group. The Group ignored the Council officers' advice that it could never sustain itself financially. All credit to the Councillors, however; they warned the Community Group that if the project failed that they would not step in to bail them out.

It had design, maintenance and on-going funding issues from the outset so was it any wonder that after three years it was a wreck, commercially unsound and closed? Jim – he's still the Council's Acting Property Manager since Farah left to have her baby - tells me that the Community Group has now surrendered the ground lease back to the Council and that he's seeking quotes to demolish the structure. The Council will then sell the cleared site for affordable housing. The Lottery Commission is livid because it can't even claim the land so that it can sell the site to offset the loss of its grant. I suspect that the Commission will be changing the national rules to require security against such assets before giving out any more grants like that.

That's the trouble with these Big Society initiatives – there are plenty of well-meaning members of the public willing to raise funds to set up these sorts of schemes but they need long term annual investment and specialist support once they're established. After the capital grant is spent there's a need to keep on fund-raising to meet the annual running costs. And those increase as the building ages. The initial volunteers are full of enthusiasm but when they move on or die there's no-one to replace them. The fundraising dries up and the schemes deteriorate from neglect. So now the community has a resort with two unused pools and a sea that no-one dares swim in because of the dangerous tides and the quick-sands.'

'How far is it to the nearest usable swimming pool?'

'As the crow flies, about eight miles across the Bay. A bit far for a swim really ... and usually cold and dangerous too whether the tide's in or out.'

They walked along the promenade back to the car park and Selwyn gave some thought as to where their next walk could take them in a couple of weeks' time, depending upon the continuing good weather.

***

'Selwyn, will you do me the honour of marrying me?

She had dropped to one knee on the sand in front

of him. Some people in the crowd turned to look and then began to applaud her.

They were in Herdwick Bay, surrounded by a backdrop of green and black fells dotted with grey lime-stone houses, at the mid-point of the old coaching route across the sands to Lantern-o'er-the-Bay, so named because in past times only the light from a big lantern lit by the villagers had helped travellers to keep to the crossing route in bad weather. To the east, west and north the empty sands stretched away under another cloudless, blue summer sky for miles in each direction before reaching landfall. To the south and out of sight but never out of mind was the sea, still held back by the pull of the moon and the tilt of the earth. Immediately in front of them was the cut where the Rivers Shep and Crook met below the head of the Bay before snaking out onto the widening sands. The cut was formed in the sands by the rivers combining and shifting position after every tide. The party needed to cross the cut to complete the second half of the walk to Lantern-o'er-the-Bay.

The Queen's Guide had marked a width with two sticks along the nearest bank of the cut and was prodding into the knee-deep, grey-brown water between those markers with his pole to determine a safe depth and a crossing free of quicksand. In a few hours the tide would come rushing back, led by a foaming, white bore travelling faster than a man could run, racing up the cut and over the rippled sands to re-fill the Bay. But for now the cross-bay walkers were safe.

Selwyn grinned and glanced at the crowd that had formed in a half-circle around him. He kissed her to a loud cheer.

'It should be me asking you.'

'Silly man, this is the age of equality. Women are allowed to do anything. We even have the right to vote now. Besides, if I waited for you to pop the question it might never happen. I've dropped you enough hints just lately.'

'Why here?'

'Well, because there are no Council properties here. This is the only place where I could be sure that you wouldn't be able to change the subject by starting one of your stories about Council property.'

'Yes, I did promise to surprise you by taking you to the only location in the district of Herdwick that's at least three miles in any direction from any parcel of Council land or any Council building. And here we are. But you're the one that's surprised me. How did you know where it was?'

'That was easy. I just rang your successor, Farah, and asked her. I knew that it would have cropped up in one of your many conversations in the years that you'd worked together. Who else but a Property Manager would know?'

'That's the thing about women' thought Selwyn, *'No matter how fast men run they're always one step ahead of us.'*

The walkers waded across the cut and walked on. From the uninterrupted viewpoint on the other bank, Selwyn pointed out, in the distance, the old Lido on the sea front and the roof of the new, soon-to-be-demolished indoor pool behind it.

'That's one of the biggest reasons that I took early retirement when it became available … daft initiatives, like the Big Society, Best Value, Asset Management Plans, Corporate Property Strategies, Key Performance Indicators … they were endless and they took the fun out of the job. That new pool was always going to fail and negotiating that ground lease was disheartening.'

'It wasn't the only reason?'

'No, my wife's illness was a big factor. Retirement helped me to look after her in the last twelve months of her life. Also, I'd stopped being a manager of property and had become a manager of surveyors. That was never something that I really wanted to do but, like everyone else, when it was offered I'd taken the promotion for the extra salary and the boost to the pension pot.'

'You wouldn't want to go back to it now, say at a lower level?'

'No, I've done my bit. After my wife died I had the time and I could have looked for a part-time post just as a surveyor and not as a manager. But that wouldn't have stopped the daft initiatives like the Big Society. Why would I want to go back and deal with things like that again? Take that new Pool for example ... it raised expectations within the Community which couldn't be realised. The local community is great at managing activities – like this Cross-Bay Walk, or Village Sports Days or Art Festivals - because they don't involve great expense or legacy issues with property after the event. They could be described as Small Society initiatives. The Bay is always here, the Guide is already employed by the Queen. The walkers just book a place on the website if they want to go, they raise sponsorship for charities, they enjoy the exercise and fresh air on the crossing and then they go home and switch off afterwards. They don't have a large building to support or staff to pay and if they lose interest then it doesn't matter if attendance drops off for a few years before being revived again by new enthusiasts. Those are small projects and easy to manage. But the community already makes those happen and they don't need a Government initiative to promote them …

… However, there's a reason that Councils exist to run those big expensive properties that don't make money, like that pool and libraries and museums and such. They employ professional help and can spread the cost across the larger population so that we all only bear a tiny share through the tax system … and all the decisions about where they're provided and what they comprise are taken democratically. The Big Society initiatives run by Community Groups may have a constitution but they don't have that in-built democratic control from across the district to mostly avoid over-reaching and costly mistakes. And so many of them fail sooner or later because they don't have the specialist expertise to sustain them indefinitely – especially in respect of property management. And they are all just ways that the Government tries to cut costs. Amateurs are always cheaper than professionals.'

'So would you describe Marriage as an activity that the Small Society should manage?' she asked, grinning at him. He knew that she was gently telling him to shut up about the pools.

'That's not a bad example actually. Generally speaking, people only pay for the wedding that they can afford, from their own resources, and the decision to proceed is always reached with a 2-0 democratic majority and afterwards on-going costs should decrease because two can usually live together cheaper than each one separately. Have you got a date in mind?'

'Not yet but I'll let you know. My legs are beginning to ache and there's nowhere dry enough to sit down for a rest out here – how far have we got to walk still?'

'About another three and a half miles ... to the Council's seats in the Council's park on the Council's promenade ... which are all still useable.'

6: PANNUS MIHI
PASSIONIS (2013)

Bernard looked every inch the prosperous businessman that farming, the Dating Agency and the Wedding Business had made him, despite the Recession. He stood with his back to an exhibition case at one end of the room and faced the interested onlookers. The spaces between exhibits in the Long Gallery on the ground floor of Shepdale Museum were packed and people were still squeezing in at the back as he started to speak.

'Good evening. I'm the Chairman of Shepdale Heritage Society and of the Friends of Shepdale Museum. Thank you for coming tonight to this combined extra-ordinary general meeting. I'm pleased to see such a large turn-out and I'd like to welcome the many new members who've recently joined. As you know, the future of the Museum is under threat and this meeting is to consider what to do about it. You will recall that Herdwick District Council is suffering from extreme austerity cuts from the Government and is forced to look at cutting non-statutory services ... things like public conveniences, parks etc ... that it is not compelled by law to provide. In particular the Council has decided that it can no longer go on supporting the Museum service. It intends to sell off those parts of the Collection that it owns outright, return those items held on loan and sell the lease of the building. We know that Shepdale College is interested in buying it.

Since the last meeting we have co-opted an expert to provide us with some estates advice and discussions have been held with the Council's Acting Property Manager. Tonight our expert, Selwyn, will report on progress and ask for your opinions. So ...'

The Shepdale Museum was located at the far end of Sheepfold Lane, the main shopping street in Shepdale. It was an imposing two storey detached limestone building with a generous basement and attics under a local slate roof. It stood in its own grounds and backed on to the Shepdale College Art Building which matched its style of construction. In his former role as Property Manager to Herdwick District Council Selwyn had managed the maintenance of the Museum building so knew it well.

Selwyn stepped forward.

'Hello. As this is a Heritage Society meeting it seems appropriate that I remind you of the history of one of Shepdale's best known characters. This is particularly relevant to the situation tonight... as you will learn. I refer, of course, to Walter Winster (1889-1945) the poet and novelist.

Walter was born in 1889 and brought up on the family sheep farm in the Shepdale Valley. As the only son, he was destined to take over the farm from his father. However, as he later related in his autobiographical novel **'Fleeced in Carlisle'**, after a drinking session in 1915 he woke up in

Carlisle Castle Barracks with a hangover to find himself enlisted in the army. In typical military fashion, because of his farming experience, he was wrongly placed as a farrier with the Army Transport Corps. He said nothing about this error because it helped to keep him out of the front line and so, despite knowing nothing about horses, he fooled the authorities just long enough for him to survive the war. On returning to Shepdale he decided that he'd seen enough of animals to last him a lifetime and took employment more suited to his interests as a barman in the Wandering Tup in Shepdale. It was during this time that he met his wife Mary (or 'Mad Mary' as she was often referred to when seen with a pick-axe shaft in her hand at throwing-out time), the daughter of his employer. They inherited the pub upon the death of her alcoholic father and had one son, Thomas, who ran away to London with the contents of the till as soon as he was tall enough to pull a pint. Walter and Mary failed to spot his absence for three days as they wrangled with Shepdale Insurance about the fire that had gutted the public bar that very same night. The cause of the fire was never established but Thomas was not seen again in Shepdale.

Despite not returning to his farming heritage Walter retained ownership of the family farm, let it out to tenants and often visited it to check on his investment. It was speculated that his lifelong interest in the wool trade stemmed from the wish for his tenants to be successful and thus keep the rent high. The rare photo in that cabinet over there shows him checking the quality of the wool of the Herdwick on his knee with his tenant at his side. It's felt that this photo was posed for a book-cover re-issue because, although he championed the wool trade in the town, he usually avoided any contact with sheep unless they were presented to him cooked on a plate.

The sale of Walter's poems and novels together with the income from the pub and the rent from the farm enabled him to lead a very comfortable life, eventually rising to become Mayor of the former Shepdale Municipal Borough Council (merged into Herdwick District Council in 1974) where he championed the Wool and Pub Trades equally in many lively and violent debates, often when the worse for drink.

His best known work, the world famous poem **'Ode to t'Erdwick'** almost earned him the appointment as 'Poet Laureate' until his prison record for drunken assault on a political opponent was revealed to the selection panel. It was written in 1919, when Walter was 30 years old, as a counterbalance to the First World War poets. It was an immediate sensation and, together with his later poems and novels, secured his international reputation as the North's greatest dialect writer. His purpose in writing was to remind people of all that was good about Britain despite the recent horrors of that war.

He saw that the simple rural life, as epitomised by the horses that he'd cared for, were being replaced by mechanical monsters like tanks capable of causing great carnage. His message was that, notwithstanding the bravery and sacrifice of the fallen, those same changes might happen in peacetime. The likely post-war rush to industrialisation caused by the conversion of the steel and armaments industries into domestic production might well sweep away the best aspects of the rural world, including shepherding on the fells. There has been much academic debate about whether he was ahead of his time or just totally wrong because sheep farming on the fells could never be mechanised and remains unchanged to this day, essentially still relying upon one man with a crook and a dog, both usually on foot. However, other aspects of rural life did eventually change with the advent of large combines, loss of hedgerows, mechanical milking, genetically modified crops etc as he had feared, although those changes did not happen until after the Second World War and, even now, it's mainly only the Green Party that sees them as necessarily bad. Notwithstanding that debate, his sentiments were aptly summed up in the Ode's immortal final lines:

"Tis t'grandest sight a man can see

Yon 'erdwicks oot on't fell.

Then us knows thars scran on't table

An' all with England's well."

His other works include the anthologies **'Fellside Musings'** where he reflects on the state of Britain between the wars (see later reference to modern politics) and its allegorical sequel **'In need of Man's Best Friend'** written just before the outbreak of World War Two and which compared the Government to a flock of sheep and suggested that the Prime Minister had less ability to organise them than a reject from a Border Collie litter.

His novels reflect his fascination with the unsavoury side of northern life. They include the very comic **'Fleeced in Carlisle'**, referred to earlier, where he describes his encounter with the violent companions of a lady of the night on a weekend trip to Carlisle's beer festival resulting in his unplanned enlistment in the army.

'A Shearer's Tale' describes the fictitious double life of an itinerant Scottish youth who shears sheep at the quiet fell farms during the week but visits the bustling cities to play professional Rugby League at weekends. In this novel the hero, young Marty, wins the Shepdale shearing championship on a Friday afternoon before cycling overnight without lights to Bradford to star in the 1935 R L Championship top-four playoff final victory at the Odsall Stadium on the Saturday. There he scores the winning try and collects his winner's bonus before disappearing with both trophies for an evening visit to a hostelry in the seedier part of Bradford accompanied by *'a blonde–haired older lady of common appearance'.*

The pair were never seen again. This later inspired the popular Pinewood Studios film **'Up fer t'Cup'**, starring a youthful Gordon Jackson, and re-enforces Winster's theme from **'Fleeced in Carlisle'** about the corrupting influence of progressive city life on an innocent country boy.

His collection of short stories entitled **'Infamous Lock-ins at the Tup'** depict the adventures of local characters who frequented his premises after closing time and has been compared favourably as a more salacious parallel to Dickens' 'Pickwick Papers'. The case against him for libel arising from one story fell apart when the litigant was found drowned and reeking of alcohol in a sheep dip on the edge of town. The Coroner recorded a verdict of probable accidental suffocation from breathing in wool fibres floating in the contaminated water. Walter and Mary gave each other an alibi for the night in question which was supported by their regulars

Walter was a man of contradictions. He was a dyed-in-the-wool Tory Councillor known to hold strong views on the sanctity of market forces above all else, particularly as regards the retail sale of alcohol. However his poems about the free-roaming Herdwicks in **'Fellside Musings'** have been credited with inspiring the modern-day environmental movement resulting in the creation of the Green Party. Also, despite his reputation as a tight-fisted publican, his interest in local history, particularly the wool trade, led him to grant the lease of the former wool warehouse on Sheepfold Lane at a peppercorn rent to the Council to house the Museum. That he had won it in a late-night poker game and that it was semi-derelict, scheduled as unsafe and in need of substantial remedial expenditure at the time may have helped influence his philanthropic decision. However, at the later enquiry which failed to reach a conclusion and thus acquitted him, he claimed that it was purely co-incidental that he had been appointed Mayor immediately following the grant of that lease and furthermore that there was absolutely no connection between that appointment and the subsequent abandonment of all discussions by the Licensing Committee regarding the Methodist-sponsored Liberal Party proposal to severely restrict the drinking hours in Shepdale and thus reduce violence in the town centre in the evenings.

Walter met his demise at the age of 56 following the disputed outcome of a bet with a customer that he could see the top of Blackpool Tower from the roof of the Wandering Tup. Witnesses in the large crowd below attested that the word 'welcher' was shouted and that both then lost their grip on the chimney stack, rolled down the roof and fell into Sheepfold Lane, with Walter landing underneath his adversary and thus unintentionally saving the other's life at the cost of his own. At his funeral, on VE day in 1945, silent crowds lined the route along Sheepfold Lane and Allhallows Road with Herdwick fleeces to muffle the sound of the horses as the funeral cortege wound its way to Allhallows Graveyard. It was an ironic twist that wool prices had plummeted overnight as orders for fleece linings for aircrews' flight suits were cancelled. Thereafter, as the Herdwick Gazette reported, customers were ten deep at the bar and spilling out onto the pavement at the Wandering Tup for the rest of the day until well after midnight and *"the local Constabulary were hard-pressed to contain them in their enthusiasm to mourn his passing whilst simultaneously celebrating the end of the War."*

Shepdale MBC's motto "Pannus mihi passionis", meaning 'wool (literally 'cloth') is my passion' was carved on his tombstone. Mary is reputed to have said later that it should have read 'wool is my brain' in relation to the manner of his death. His works still continue to sell in small numbers, particularly in Brighton.

When Walter had granted the Lease of the Museum building to the Council he included the following terms and conditions:

- The term to be for 999 years from 1st September 1935.

- The rent to be one shilling (now 5 new pence) per annum payable yearly in advance as and when demanded and without review.

- The building not to be used other than as a museum for the enjoyment and education of the residents of Shepdale and for no other purpose whatsoever.

- The Council to covenant to put the building into good and tenantable repair at the commencement of the lease and to maintain it as such thereafter.

- The Council not to make any alterations or improvements to the building without the consent of the Landlord.

- The Council to meet all running costs and outgoings in respect of the property.

After Walter's death Mary sold the farm and the pub and was rumoured to have gone to London in search of Thomas. No rent for the Museum has ever been collected by Walter or his descendants. No one knows who inherited the benefit of the ownership of the freehold from Walter. So the Council has formed the view that it can sell the lease for alternative commercial use because it is unlikely that anyone with a direct interest will come forward to challenge its proposal and, it believes, it can arrange realistic Forfeiture of Lease (Breach of Covenant) insurance against such an unlikely occurrence.

However, we have discovered some information which may well frustrate the Council's plans.

Bernard, your Chairman, farms sheep up the Shepdale Valley. His neighbour runs the adjoining farm, the one with a guesthouse and the small Herdwick Visitor Centre. Recently he mentioned to Bernard that, last year, one of his guests was called John Winster, that he lived in London and that he'd claimed to be the only grandchild of Walter, visiting to research his family tree. He'd stayed at that farm because it had been the Winster family farm. When the Council's threat to the Museum made the front page of the Herdwick Gazette, Bernard had the presence of mind to mention this information to me. I have contacted John, seen his research and also confirmed with the Publishers that all royalties for Walter's writing are being paid to John following the death of his father, Thomas, until the copyright expires in 2015.

The Solicitor for Herdwick District Council accepts that John is the current Landlord of the Museum building. He's advised the Council that it won't be possible to sell the Lease for any other use without consent from John Winster. However, it can still sell the Collection, mothball the building and make a partial saving that way. John's come up from London today and I will ask him to say a few words.'

'Hello. Until recently I'd no idea that there was a lease for this building, never mind that I was the Landlord. The Council has asked me for consent to change the use of the building to commercial purposes to allow them to sell the Lease. I'm minded to refuse.'

A cheer went up from the audience.

'However, the Council is still in a difficult financial position and I would like to help them if they can come up with a reasonable solution which also includes retaining the Museum use. Now Selwyn will explain how that can be achieved.'

Selwyn continued.

'I've met with Jim, the Council's Acting Property Manager, and the Principal of Shepdale College. Between us we've reached a provisional deal for the College to take over the management of the Museum on a charge-free basis but to keep it open as a Museum at least for the next ten years. There will be sharing of the accommodation with Art courses using the facilities for life and still-life drawing, craft and textile studies, printing and exhibition skills and any other educational interests where the two uses overlap including evening classes for the community. All running costs will be shared on a proportionate basis according to usage. Studies will take place in the mornings and the Museum will be open to the public in the afternoons. The staff will transfer to the College, keep their curating duties part-time and become part-time lecturers on a new Master's Degree in Curating, generating income from students from home and abroad. All parties have to approve the deal but first we want to know what you think about it.'

***

Jim was waiting for them in a booth seat in the Tup. John Winster and Selwyn joined him whilst Bernard went to the bar to buy a round. Others from the meeting trickled into the pub behind them.

'How did it go? Is there support for the deal?'

'I think that you can be pretty optimistic,' replied Selwyn. 'Although you don't strictly need the agreement of the Society and the Friends, as they're not parties to the Lease, everyone was generally in support. It's a win, win, win situation. The Councillors will be pleased that they have made a substantial cost saving and they can present themselves as saviours of the Museum at the next election. The Art College will be happy at securing the shared use of new facilities and the Museum can look forward to a continuing future. It's all down to John here who's saved the day.'

'Thanks, but you people did all the work. I just supported what seemed to me to be a fair and sensible proposal. But Selwyn ... there's one thing that still bothers me.'

'What's that?'

'Can you really see Blackpool Tower off the roof of this building? Did Walter Winster win his wager?'

'I can tell from that alliteration that you've inherited some of your grandad's literary talent. My honest answer is, I don't know. But I can tell thee summat fer nowt. I wouldn't bet my life on it.'

7: DUE DILIGENCE (2017/18)

E-mail sent at 11:43 on 15 November 2017.

Re: Property Group Christmas Lunch

Hi Selwyn,

As you know I've been back at Herdwick District Council, but in my new part-time job as Client Property Manager, for the past 18 months since Jim retired.

I know that you're still interested in events within your old Property Group. There are big changes planned for us from April 2018. I'll fill you in on some of the details when I see you.

Hopefully that will be at the Christmas Lunch on Friday 15 December 2017 at 12.00 in the Wandering Tup in Shepdale Town Centre. This is your formal invitation. A menu is attached. Please let me know if you can come and which three courses you want me to pre-order for you. The cost is £20 payable on the day. There are still quite a few old colleagues here that remember you. They are looking forward to seeing you. Jim has confirmed that he will attend.

Best wishes, Farah

***

The 15th of December came around quickly. The Christmas decorations lit up Sheepfold Lane, the main shopping street, on what was a very dark day. They were a credit to the Town Centre Manager's efforts and gave the street a festive atmosphere despite the clouds that threatened further rain showers. The town centre was full of shoppers but Selwyn still managed to find a space in the yard at the back of the pub as most of the Tup's customers had walked there from the Council offices opposite. Jim beckoned to him from the bar on the far side of the crowded room and gestured towards the pump marked 'Rampant Ram'. Selwyn nodded and mouthed *'a half'* to him as he weaved his way through the throng, greeting old friends and Council colleagues. Along the way Farah grabbed his sleeve.

'Hello stranger. You haven't been to see me for quite a while.'

'I don't like to keep disturbing you now that you're back at work. You're a busy woman. But, I am intrigued. What are the big changes that you mentioned in your e-mail?'

'You've probably heard that the Property and Design Groups are being outsourced. Well things have moved on. The Council ran a two-stage tender. The first stage was to invite interest from outside firms and assess them on ability to do the job and on quality. The second stage was to invite those that made it onto the 'quality' shortlist to bid on price to see what each would charge for providing the combined Service. The second stage bids have been evaluated and the Council's Cabinet will formally approve the winner at next week's meeting. We expect to sign contracts in January.'

'What will happen to the current staff?'

'They will all transfer to the winning contractor under European TUPE rules so their existing pay and conditions will be protected, at least initially.'

'When will the new contract start?'

'From next April.'

'Will you be transferring as part of the deal?'

'Not likely. When Jim retired the Council merged the Design and Property Services Groups. Then they split the two manager's jobs into a Client role and a Contractor role ready for outsourcing the work. They put an Architect in charge of the contractor side to deliver the combined service and advertised for a Client Property Manager to monitor the contract. I applied and was appointed to that job. When the outsourcing is complete the Council wants me to stay with them as that internal Client Manager running the contract from their side; checking that the contractor delivers what's required under that contract. That suits me better; I can still help Sadiq with our IT business for two days as my Council job is only 3 days per week and the kids are now in school and nursery respectively so I have more free time when I'm at home. It's working well.

'Who's the winning contractor?'

'I can't tell you that just yet. It's confidential, although I expect that you will soon know as the Council still leaks like a sieve. I shouldn't be surprised if someone else whispers it to you before this meal ends today. Just as long as it can't be attributed to me.'

***

Selwyn felt good. The meal had been excellent. He'd stuck to orange juice after that first half of Rampant so as not to risk his driving licence and he needed to stay alert for the opportunity that would likely occur at some point during the proceedings. He'd enjoyed catching up with Farah and his other ex-colleagues. Not surprisingly, the conversation had been dominated by talk of the outsourcing. All through the meal he had counted the pints that Eric from the Finance Group had been drinking at their parallel gathering on another table. Now, as most people were saying goodbye and drifting back to work, Selwyn saw his chance.

Eric stepped back from the urinal with his hands occupied, misjudged the step down and staggered slightly before catching his balance.

'I shouldn't have had that last pint, Selwyn.'

'You shouldn't have had the other four either,' thought Selwyn.

He hoped that Eric would not be adding up any columns of figures at work later that day or there could be a bit of a hole in the Council's finances. Not that there would be much work done by anyone in the Council offices that afternoon.

'Still working then? How's life in Finance? You must be getting near retirement age now, surely?'

'Only another year near to go, thank god. Then you won't see me for dust.'

'I hear that you were on the evaluation panel for the Property and Design Service bids. It's all anyone can talk about on our table today. I'm glad that I'm retired and well out of it.'

'It's the beginning of the end.'

'Sorry, what do you mean by that exactly?'

'This is just between us, ok?'

He leaned across and whispered in Selwyn's ear, 'They are being recommended to award it to ...'

'And have they passed the due diligence scrutiny?'

'Oh yes. They are a big – well probably the biggest - firm of Building, Civil Engineering and Public Sector Service Contractors certainly in this country and they are pretty big internationally too. They have a huge amount of Central Government and Local Government contracts in place as well as big contracts abroad. They already run prison services and hospitals and academies in the UK. The Government awarded them another couple more contracts in November which shows the confidence that Westminster has in them. But our Director of Finance covered his back. He thought that the checking was a bit above the skills of us mere mortals in the Finance Department so he paid a small fortune in fees to a big City accountancy firm to advise the Council. But these Contractors are so big so how could anyone doubt that they're financially sound?'

Selwyn thought that he detected a hint of sarcasm in that last remark but let it go.

'But why is a huge firm like that interested in little Herdwick District Council?'

'We asked that question. Lots of reasons. The official answers - they like to spread their interests across a lot of different sized contracts to minimise the risk for them and so protect their clients. The wide range of skills available across their numerous contracts means that they can move staff around where they are needed most and that benefits all their clients. Also, it helps their public image - they can claim that they are putting something back into the community if they assist small clients as well as large ones. They say that anything that adds to their size produces economies of scale which means that they can pretty much beat any other competitor on price so why shouldn't small clients benefit from that as well as big clients. They already have a regional presence so they won't need a top management layer as we can fit within their model.   There you have them - lots of waffley reasons. And they claim that they can still make their margin whilst providing savings for the Council through some profit-share arrangement. It looks great in a bid statement. The Councillors swallowed it. Farah spoke against it but they just ignored her. It was the same in your day, wasn't it? The Councillors always ignore the internal opinion in favour of the outsiders, especially when they've paid a fortune for that advice.'

'And the unofficial answer?'

'They want a toe-hold in this part of the north west. They're not really interested in the Property and Design Service on its own - that's just a start. If they can show savings on costs for the Council and pump in staff from other offices to meet peak workloads to solve our recruitment crisis then the Councillors will think that they're wonderful. The Contractor thinks that will open the door to more contracts for other services. Then they can take over the running of the whole Council and then the word will spread out into other neighbouring Councils. In a few years' time they expect to be running the whole County.'

***

Selwyn and Jim had followed Farah across to her room in the Council offices behind the Town Hall for a coffee. They closed the door behind them.

'I have my doubts about this whole thing but nobody within the Council wants to listen to me. It could all end in tears. Luckily there's a need for an internal Client Manager role, as I told you, so I'm fairly safe. However I still feel a bit guilty about the others who will transfer across. The risk to their pensions alone if they're transferred into the Contractor's scheme must be a big concern for them.'

'I know how you feel Farah. I'd be just as concerned for them if I was still working. We can only hope for the best. Thank god that we're out of it, eh Jim?'

'Amen to that.'

***

It was another cold, wet January day and Selwyn was lingering over his breakfast trying to put off the time when he'd have to go outside to the car.

'Come on, let's get going. I got some vouchers for Christmas and I want to spend them in the sales. You can drop me off at the Sheepfold Shopping Centre and go for a wander round on your own to see what changes have happened to your old property empire. Better still - you should ring Jim and ask him to join you. He's often at a loose end when he can't play golf in the winter. I know how much you enjoy chatting to him about the old days. I'll never understand how you can get so much pleasure from looking at those old buildings. Speaking of old buildings, it's almost the anniversary of the day when I met you walking up to Reservoir Cottage with your capacious briefcase. We can celebrate that with lunch in the Tup when you've finished your tour of inspection.'

Selwyn smiled at his wife and reached for the remote to switch off the BBC news.

'I just like to see what changes are going on. I have so many memories tied up in those properties.'

As he pointed the remote a familiar sounding name caught his attention:

'... the massive Construction and Public Service Contractor is on the brink of financial collapse. There are concerns for the fate of its employees and those reliant upon the pension fund which has a significant shortfall in its balances. It is likely that the Receivers will be called in if urgent meetings with the Minister do not produce a solution later today. Questions are already being asked by the Opposition about what will happen to their existing public service contracts and why the Government awarded further large contracts to them as late as last November if their finances were as precarious then as is being reported now ...'

Selwyn pressed the off button and walked through into the hallway to collect his coat and car keys. Perhaps he'd stick his head around Farah's office door, just for a couple of minutes whilst he was in Shepdale Town Centre, and get her take on the news. He could congratulate her on her astute assessment of the risk. It would be something to talk to Jim about.

'Hopefully the Council still has time to pull back from the brink, he thought, *'whilst Jim and I, on the other hand, still have all the time in the world to dissect it over a pint of Rampant Ram in the Wandering Tup.'*

8: A MAN OF PROPERTY (2018)

'For we brought nothing into this world, and it is certain we can carry nothing out.'

The Vicar of Allhallows Church was reaching the end of the service. The group of about thirty people standing around the open graveside shuffled their umbrellas and some turned to walk away. Others queued to pick up small amounts of dry earth from a box held out by the Undertaker and gently tossed them onto the lowered coffin as they passed. All of them were keen to get out of the relentless drizzle.

Jim, the retired former Senior Committee Clerk and Acting Property Manager for Herdwick District Council, cleared his throat and announced to the gathering,

'If anyone wishes to come, there're sandwiches and refreshments provided down the road at the Wandering Tup. All are welcome.'

From the graveyard he could look down across the top of the town and see the Clock Tower on Shepdale Town Hall and, opposite to it on the main shopping street, the grey, slate roof of the Wandering Tup, the oldest pub in Shepdale. Beyond them the hills on the far side of the valley provided a darker backdrop, almost invisible in the dullness of the day.

Farah, the current Client Property Manager for the Council, linked arms with him and together they followed the small throng of existing and past Council colleagues and friends down Allhallows Road to the pub.

'It's a very appropriate view for him,' he said. 'From here he'll be able to look down forever on the two places that he frequented the most – the place where he earned his salary and the place where he spent most of it.'

***

'It's on days like these that I wish Selwyn was here.'

'Me too, Farah ... me too. Still, I worked with him for so long that I now know enough stories about characters in the Council to enable me to put together a eulogy without having to rely upon him?'

They were sat in a booth in the main bar of the Tup. It was still too early for the lunchtime trade. Jim had a pint of Rampant Ram and Farah had her usual water. The other mourners mingled around them, collecting their drinks at the small bar, queuing at the buffet, which was spread on a white table-cloth over a board which covered the whole of the pool table, or speaking quietly in twos and threes seated at the scattered tables. A log fire hissed and crackled in a fireplace to one side of the room. The iron umbrella rack near to it was filled with umbrellas, steaming as they dried out.

'Jim, how come you ended up with the job of organising everything else as well as giving the eulogy?' Farah asked him.

'Basically there was no-one else. I received a request to go and see him when they were giving him end-of-life-care in the Hospice. He'd no remaining relatives, lived on his own and apparently his only friends were those of us that worked with him but who only saw him at work or the stalwarts who lined the bar of the Tup to drink with him every night. When I visited him he asked me to be the Executor of his Will and to organise this do. His instructions were to sell his entire estate and, after expenses, to divide the proceeds equally between the Hospice and the British Liver Trust. He was on a transplant list for a new liver but he ran out of time before they could find a suitable donor.'

'It's such a pity that he never got to enjoy his retirement.'

'Did you hear what the Vicar was saying at the graveyard earlier? Something about we come into this world with nothing and we leave with nothing. It's a quote from Timothy 6:7 in the Bible – I looked it up once. I don't know if you have the equivalent expression in the Quran. It's a standard part of the Christian burial service. Selwyn once told me that he didn't agree with that particular statement. He thought that there was one property exception to that rule.

'Selwyn has a theory for everything, especially if it involves property.'

'Do you remember when old Cedric Symons died in the Council Chamber in 2002? Well he was buried in the municipal Cemetery at Winander up by the lakeshore road. Selwyn and Eric and I went to that funeral. You manage its maintenance, Farah, and it's part of the Asset Valuations work so you must have seen it on your travels. It's a modern cemetery, unlike all the others managed by the Council, with plenty of room for future burials. The reason for it being modern is that it replaced the old Cemetery further down the road which had to be moved. That was in the late 1970s when we had those prolonged and heavy rainstorms. I was just an Admin Officer in those days. The lake was on the low side of the road and the cemetery was on the high side with Winander Ghyll running through it and discharging into the lake via a culvert under the road. The volume of water coming down the Ghyll was so large that the road collapsed and a big part of the cemetery slid down the hill, exposing skeletons and coffins all over the place. The road was closed for ages and temporary road diversions had to be put in place using the narrow back lanes to get around it. It took about five years to sort it all out finally with a permanent solution. The road diversions were a real pain for the locals, especially in summer when the tourists arrived.

The County Council as highway authority had to clean it all up and sort out the road because it was their wall and culvert that'd collapsed. They decided that the best solution was to ask Herdwick District Council to move the cemetery to a new location, cut a chunk out of the hillside and then construct a massive new retaining wall and insert a new wider culvert under the road to prevent flood debris building up and so happening again. They needed the District Council's cooperation in respect of the Cemetery land. Selwyn had to buy a nearby field for the replacement Cemetery, so he bought a big one to build-in extra capacity, so they could then transfer the bodies and sell the old Cemetery land to the County. Effectively the County had to pick up the bill for the new Cemetery and the specialist cost of relocating all the bodies from the old one. Selwyn was just a young Estates Surveyor then, not the Property Manager, but he was put in charge of a small team for the project. He had an Architect to design the new Cemetery and manage the works, help from Keith the HDC Cemeteries Officer with planning it out from the burial records and the project budgeting and accounting was done by Eric, who was just a young accountant on his first job with the Council. Selwyn and Eric told me that they learnt a lot about Cemeteries from that job.

Anyway, after we'd buried Cedric - I remember it was raining just like today – I can never remember going to a sunny funeral in my entire life - we all went for a pint in the Winander Arms and that's when Selwyn outlined his theory to us. Selwyn's point was that some of the dead have rights. They might have lost their lives and had all their possessions and wealth and status stripped away from them to be passed on to relatives after death but if they'd purchased a plot and exercised a burial certificate then they would have possession of a grave which nobody could take away from them, not even if the Cemetery was destroyed. All those old bodies at Winander had to be relocated to new plots in the replacement Cemetery based on Keith's original plan. Selwyn reckoned that whilst *'we can carry nothing out'* covered most cases, especially cremations, it failed to take into account burial rights – if the dead were in possession of the land then they were left with it permanently ... or at least for a very long time. His rather macabre comment – which was the reason that it popped into my mind today at the graveside when I was listening to the Vicar - was that *"even a corpse can be a man of property."* That would apply to our friend today.'

They laughed and then lapsed into silence to reflect upon Selwyn's theory.

As if on cue the door to the back room opened and Selwyn entered, removing his raincoat and shaking off the raindrops onto the carpet.

'Hello everyone. I'm sorry that I missed the funeral. We've just got off the train and my wife has taken our suitcases home in the taxi. I rushed here as quickly as I could in the hope of catching you before you left. How did it go Jim?'

'It went as well as could be expected for a funeral. The weather could have been better. Eric's in the ground and those that turned out are all in here drinking to his memory. Go and get yourself a pint of Rampant from the bar … it's paid for by Eric.'

Selwyn returned with his pint and sat down with them.

'Here's to Eric. He was a good bloke.' They clinked glasses and echoed his sentiment.

Farah looked at Selwyn. 'It's good to have you back. How was the holiday?'

'Great, we enjoyed ourselves. I'm not sure that I'd want to go there again though. Two weeks of sun, sea and sangria was enough for me. We resisted the urge to buy a time-share interest. I think that I'd like to try somewhere else next time, just for the variety.'

'Quite right,' said Jim, smiling. 'You don't want to be investing in property at your time of life. You can't take it with you when you go.'

9: THE GOLDEN FLEECE (2036)

The time line on the conspicuous and somewhat inappropriate digital screen attached to the first-floor balcony at the front of Shepdale's Victorian Town Hall scrolled across:

20:59 Tuesday 6 September 2036: *... Breaking News ... Herdwick District Council resolves to transfer Council offices to Herdwick Powersource plc for global sales centre ...*

Farah walked through the automatic doors below the screen and saw Selwyn and his companion sitting on one of two public seats facing the Town Hall. Otherwise, the seats were empty. The fine summer weather had continued on into September but darkness was now descending, triggering the streetlights. Even on that warm, dry evening the rest of the street was deserted apart from the occasional passengers disembarking from the Driverless Taxis (DLTs) and heading for the "Tuesday night Mutton Curry and pint of Rampant Ram meal deal" in the Wandering Tup on the opposite side of the street from the Town Hall. The emptied taxis glided silently over the head of the pedestrian area that now included the section of Sheepfold Lane north of the Town Hall crossroads where Selwyn was sat, and returned to their parking bays. The Lane was still the main commercial street in Shepdale but banks, shops and offices had become relatively scarce since the boom in home-working and on-line trading. Cafés, restaurants and convenience stores still occasionally filled the frontages but increasingly the lights that shone and the television screens that flickered were from behind the closed curtains at the windows of the affordable flats conversions comprising the main use for the bulk of the old limestone town centre buildings.

'Hello Selwyn, hello Bob. Have you been waiting for me? How did you know I was here? Does anyone know where you are?'

Before Selwyn could answer a silent drone dropped down from the sky and hovered nearby at head height. A hologram of a police constable beamed down to stand facing them.

'Good evening ma'am, good evening sir. I'm PC Johnson currently in Shepdale Police Station. Do you require any assistance? If so, I can have someone with you in less than five minutes.'

'I'm just checking constable. I'll make a phone call. Please bear with me.'

Farah turned away, dialled a number and spoke into the phone. Then she turned back and said,

'There's no real problem. I've spoken to his wife' – she gestured towards Selwyn. 'They've been out all day but I've confirmed that Selwyn has checked in with her by phone at regular intervals. She's asked that I put them into a DLT and program it to return them home before too long. Thank you for your offer of help but we don't need it.'

'That's ok ma'am. I've done a retinal scan and there's no record of any of you being reported as missing so I'll leave these two in your capable hands. Have a good evening.'

The hologram extinguished itself and the drone lifted clear of the rooftops to resume its patrol.

'No, I didn't know you were here. Bob and I have just been on a tour of the old haunts, reliving the past. But it's good to see you. Actually, I'm surprised to see you here as I thought that all Council business was conducted from home by digital tele-conferencing these days.'

'It is but my portable DTC unit went on the blink at the last minute so, to be on the safe side, I came into the 24 hour Town Hall Tech Centre to use the facilities here for tonight's meeting. I could have linked in with my phone instead but it was a nice evening for a walk. You can see the outcome on the news screen up there.'

'Yes, you're transferring our old offices. What's

the plan for them? In fact, what's it like to be the high-powered Chief Executive of the richest Council in Britain?'

'Well, it's very busy, especially as I also have the Council's partnership seat on the Board of Herdwick Powersource, but it's a lot less hassle than when we used to work together at the Council in the good, or was it the bad, old days.'

'Shouldn't you be thinking about retirement soon?'

'Yes, it's been on my mind recently. It's probably best to go out at the top.'

'How things seem to have changed for the better. It's unbelievable how fast the time has gone. I always knew that you would do well Farah and you deserved your promotion to Chief Executive. You always had great insight, as you proved when you eventually persuaded the Council not to outsource the Property and Design Services all those years ago. But this Herdwick Powersource venture is out of all proportion to what I expected, even from you. And, every credit to you. You were the only one to spot the opportunity when young Philip returned from Manchester University with his big idea. No-one else would back him then but you opened the door and welcomed him in. We've been to see his dad, Bernard, earlier today. He's very proud of

Philip's success. Retired now of course, but still living in a cottage up the Shepdale Valley. He's sold off the Wedding and Dating Agency business and most of the farm to one of his neighbours but he's still running a few sheep as a very profitable hobby and Bob always finds that interesting when we visit.'

'I seem to remember that it was a joint effort. Bernard asked you first for advice for Philip about obtaining business premises to relocate his early struggles from one of Bernard's barns. You then steered him towards me at the Council to explore that longstanding rural business support initiative that we set up in the 1990s when you were my boss in Property Services.'

'It's kind of you to say so but, let's be honest, it was you that saw the potential. I was just passing Philip on.'

'Anyway, to answer your original question. The plan, after tonight's favourable decision, is that Herdwick Powersource will move its tele-sales team out of the industrial estate. The team needs more floor space and better IT connections quickly, which they can get from being in the empty Council offices near to the Town Hall Tech Centre. They need to stay in contact with their international customers and their world-wide licensees and franchisees. That will allow the manufacturing department to expand within the industrial estate to help meet British demand. The rest of the world is serviced from its subsidiaries abroad, of course.'

'I suppose the high-paid tech jobs have been a big boost for the local economy but to get Council tax down to zero and still be able to finance all the local services expenditure, underpin all those local social improvements and set up a sinking fund for all corporate property maintenance on top must make you the envy of the country. I should imagine the Government is very pleased.'

'To some extent. They like the way our exports and franchising and such have reversed the national Balance of Payments deficit but they still give us problems. It was ok when we were small and no-one knew what the potential was. Philip came in one day with his idea to develop his everlasting, self-generating energy cells, or batteries as I still prefer to call them. To quote the sales blurb, each battery is a nano-sized cold fusion reactor forcing hydrogen atoms together from deuterium extracted from water encased in a leak-proof, indestructible casing of Graphene blended with Herdwick wool fibres. I still don't understand the science but apparently the wool's unique insulating qualities can't be bettered to prevent heat and energy loss within each unit – after all it keeps the sheep alive in sub-zero temperatures under the snow drifts - and that allows the contained energy generation not only to sustain itself but also to produce surplus electricity indefinitely and at no cost. Each unit is environmentally-friendly, gives off no harmful emissions and if it should ever degrade, which is unlikely, it's completely safe because it simply stops generating, and they can all be recycled. We can make units to any size and shape from a pin-head to a shoe-box and, simply by linking enough of them together like Lego bricks, we can power anything from a single LED to the National Grid. Not that we really need much of a National Grid anymore now that we can incorporate them into the casings of each self-powering electrical product.'

'I remember – nobody else would touch Philip with a barge-pole at that time. You just thought what has the Council got to lose and gave him the lease of a free factory together with a rural enterprise grant. I seem to recall that the lease was for less than 7 years to exempt it from the best consideration requirements of Section 123 of the Local Government Act 1972 – see I can still remember the legislation after all this time even though I can't remember what I had for breakfast this morning - on the basis that he gave the Council a 25% stake in the business once it became profitable. You persuaded the Councillors, Philip delivered the goods and now Herdwick District is to the world's energy economy what Silicon Valley is to computers.'

'It worked out well, Selwyn. Today those batteries literally power everything across the world, undersea and in space – that drone, the DLTs, those street lights, those flickering TVs, the Town Hall Tech Centre with its digital screen, that armada of satellites and International Space Stations passing overhead - and we can't make enough of them. It's a global company that's bigger than Amazon, Google and Microsoft added together. And what really pleases me the most - the sheep farmers are back in business in a big way. Who would have thought that Herdwick wool – that once cost more to shear than it was worth to sell - would turn out to be the Golden Fleece? The Government's not really happy that the Council is now financially independent of them and so pretty much beyond their control - apparently London is no longer the wealth centre of the country in comparison to the Northern Powerhouse - but there's not much that they can do about it.'

'Bob and I had a look at some of the Council's property improvements today. We took a tour in a DLT using my pensioners' free-travel app. I wouldn't want to be Chief Exec like you but I wish that I was young and starting out as Property Manager again but this time with your resources. That new glass dome over Lantern Lido and the massive refurb of the inside to provide the combined pool, sports complex and indoor arena is very impressive. The wrinklies must be pleased. The new Bay Bridge road and rail links are excellent, especially with the disabled access and glass viewing facilities over the sea for those who can't enjoy the old coach crossing route over the sands. The Museum extension with the 'History of Herdwicks' exhibition is very appropriate and interesting. Bob and I even tried out one your many high-level cable car routes today - the main one up the Shepdale Valley that includes a stop near Bernard's place - rather than be driven up there in the DLT. The views from that height are magnificent and I've never seen so many sheep on the fells. We can thank chips with unique indelible genetic barcodes – or should that be *baa-codes* - and satellite tracking for allowing us to account for each one even if the rustlers get past the initial drone patrols. And they all look so fit and well; presumably that's a tribute to the selective breeding programmes. It's fine using the cable route in the summer but my days of walking up there in the snow are long gone unfortunately. Still, it did bring back pleasant memories of that time when I first met my then wife-to-be on the track to Reservoir Cottage.'

'Have you eaten?'

'Yes thanks. Bob and I went into the Wandering Tup in late afternoon when we got back down here. I had a pint of Rampant and a mint and mutton sandwich and Bob had the special - a cold mutton pie - with his still water. You can't get lamb any more as they're all out on the fells growing wool. The mid-week lunchtime trade seems to have dropped off following the closure of the Council offices and the main shops but the Landlord tells me that the residents from the nearby flats now fill it up over the new three-day weekends. It was very pleasant but we didn't stop long as there was no-one in there that we knew. That's the trouble with growing old, you outlive most of your friends. Anyway, we'll be heading home now, I'm starting to feel very tired and I've got a bit of a headache coming on. Too much fresh air I expect.'

'I'll summon a DLT for you.'

She pointed her phone at the line of taxies parked in the bays further up the pedestrian area. The lights on the nearest DLT blinked on and it reversed out beeping a warning, and then turned and drove slowly towards them before stopping. The gull wing doors lifted open. Farah checked her phone contacts for Selwyn's details, leaned in and tapped his postcode into the dashboard display and, as an afterthought, pressed the security button which disabled the passenger steering option and which, barring rare impacts or optional manual override, only allowed the doors to open upon termination of the fixed journey.

Selwyn raised himself from the seat and, leaning on his walking stick, hobbled over to the DLT. Bob scuttled past him, hopped into the passenger foot-well and settled down there. Selwyn turned and hugged Farah before clambering in after him.

'Are you coming,' he said.

'No I'm walking home. It's not far.'

'Sorry but I wasn't asking you. I was talking to those three sat on that other seat. You remember Jim, who filled in for you when you took your career break to bring up your kids, and Eric from Finance who did our accounts ... and please say hello to Arthur my old boss. All men of property now. They keep me company on my outings these days. I can't get much conversation out of Bob and he's too young to remember the past anyway.'

Farah looked at the empty seat and frowned.

'But there's no-one ... They are all ...' She stopped herself. 'Never mind. Will you be all right?'

'Don't worry, I'll be ok. It's time to go. Goodbye and, as I don't know when I'll see you again, please let me say that you've done very well and that I'm proud of you. Not many Property Managers get to be Chief Executive. We speak our minds too openly for the politicians to favour us. Now, take that retirement and enjoy the rest of your life.'

She stepped away from the sensors and the doors dropped down into position as the seat belts automatically encircled him. The DLT detected his contactless travel app on the phone within his jacket pocket, said 'Free transaction recorded' and eased itself away from Farah into the nearest traffic lane.

She pulled out her phone again as she watched him go.

'He's on his way home with Bob. He's very tired and his mind seems to be rambling a bit. I know you've mentioned it before but I just thought that I should let you know. He'll be with you in about fifteen minutes so can you please keep a look-out for him?'

Selwyn sat back and closed his eyes. It had been a good day but the headache was worsening now. His arm fell loose, the side of his face drooped and his head lolled over until it rested against the door window glass. The Collie sat up in the foot-well, looked at him and let out a single low howl – just like the one he'd howled the day that Jim had collapsed when out walking him around the edge of the golf course, before Bob had gone to live with Selwyn.

The DLT said,

'I'm sorry but I cannot accept that verbal instruction. The security locks are in place. Please press Override if you wish to cancel the pre-set journey.'

Selwyn never moved. Bob rested his jaw on Selwyn's knee and studied the faces of the four silent passengers for the rest of the journey home.

10: A WELL-KNOWN LOCAL CHARACTER (2036)

'Thanks for the water. What are you drinking? Rampant Ram just like your father ... although Selwyn would have had a pint not a half of course.'

They laughed.

'Yes he liked the local ale.'

Farah, the current Chief Executive and former Property Services Manager of Herdwick District Council and Lisa, Selwyn's daughter from his first marriage, were seated in the front window booth of the Wandering Tup on Sheepfold Lane looking across at Shepdale Town Hall. It was sunny for the time of year and the street was crowded with shoppers, office workers seeking lunch and late-season tourists following the Walter Winster town trail before dispersing to the fells to marvel at the unique Herdwick sheep which now played such an important role in saving the planet. The timeline on the electronic banner running across the Town Hall's first floor balcony was on a loop reading:

***12:25 Friday 24 October 2036**: ... Breaking News ... Shepdale Museum honours well-known local* *character...*

Farah nodded towards the timeline and said, 'He deserves the honour.'

'No doubt you had a lot to do with it?'

'Well, he was my mentor but it wasn't my idea. However, when the Friends of Shepdale Museum raised it I was happy to help. Herdwick District doesn't have a lot of famous sons or daughters to choose from so why not honour the ones it has. There's Walter Winster, the world-famous Herdwick dialect poet of course, who fell off the roof of this very pub and is reckoned to still haunt it. And there's Philip, who is still very much alive as Managing Director of Herdwick Powersource. His development of the nuclear fusion battery, thereby single-handedly saving the planet, will earn him his place in history. So he deserves to be there after his death but he's far too young to be history yet. And that's about it. Let's face it, the big world events have pretty-much passed Herdwick by. But history can be modern as well as old, and of local as well as national importance, so why not an exhibition about one of its well-known local characters?'

'But Dad's fame isn't really in the same league as those others. He spent all his working life at the Council, but others have done that too ... you included, apart from your maternity breaks. He wrote a few fell-walking guide books which gained him the nick-name 'Pilot of the Fells' and generated a bit of national interest, but that's about all.'

'No matter. That's enough to be famous in Herdwick and I think it's fitting that they honour Selwyn. After all, people in Westminster have been granted knighthoods for less effort. He also did lots of other things – training loads of student surveyors, including me, over the years, coming back to help out with the asset valuations after he retired, helping save the museum. When you think about it he did lots for the community on the quiet.'

'Well I suppose so. He'd appreciate you saying that even though Dad would be amazed and, most likely, too embarrassed to admit it.'

'What happened to Bob, Selwyn's old collie?'

'My stepmother was too old to exercise him. He went to spend his retirement with Bernard on the farm up in the Shepdale Valley. Plenty of sheep for him to watch up there. He seems quite happy.'

'So what have you brought for me? I recognise his old briefcase.'

Lisa made a space between the drinks, hoisted it off the floor and plonked it on the table.

'After Dad's funeral my stepmother invited me up to go through his possessions and said that I could take any personal items of his that I might like. This was lodged in the bottom of a wardrobe. When you mentioned that the museum was looking for exhibits I thought that its contents summed up Dad admirably.'

Lisa opened it up and began to describe the contents as she placed each of them on the table.

'There's his old 'Associate' and 'Fellow' Chartered Surveying certificates which he refused to send back to the Royal Institution on principle after terminating his membership following his early retirement in 2003. He said he was keeping them as they'd been more-than-paid-for through annual membership fees for in excess of 30 years.

There's a well-thumbed copy of Parry's Valuation Tables 1966 Edition with tax supplement at 8 shillings & threepence in the £, which he must have bought as a student.

Also, his last photo-identity badge from his Herdwick District Council days.

You'll probably recognise those items tied in a bundle with pink deed-parcel string. They're an assortment of imperial and metric scale-rulers which appear to be his career-long collection judging by the faded colours and worn graduations on some of them. That small, wooden one looks ancient.

There's a solar-powered Sanyo calculator, I guess from the 1980's, because he hated relying on anything that needed replacement batteries. Remarkably, it still works and has a small handwritten booklet of imperial/metric conversion tables for area, distance, volume etc cut to tuck inside its case.

We also have two matching leather-cased 100-feet Rabone Chesterman imperial/decimal tape measures. He was never comfortable with the laser gadgets. One tape measure has 'Buying' written on it and 'Selling' is written on the other in indelible ink. You must have heard him tell that old surveying joke about these; that one was shorter than the other depending upon what the job entailed.'

Farah laughed. 'Yes, I remember him catching me out with that when I first started as his trainee. How he laughed at my gullibility when I believed him.'

'The envelope contains some old photos of Dad with various people at presentations and leaving-dos. You'll recognise a younger you on some of them. There's an early one with his old boss Arthur and some with his drinking mates Jim and Eric and others. Most of them died before he did.

I've also brought a set of the signed, first-edition guide books that must have been presented to him by the Herdwick Gazette when they originally printed them. They may be worth a few bob now but I'd rather put them on permanent loan at the Museum for anyone to see rather than lock them away in a cupboard. These are what earned him that "Pilot of the Fells" nickname.'

Farah smiled and nodded, 'They were before my time. He must have walked every footpath and fell in Herdwick when he was a young surveyor in the sixties and seventies and later – hence the titles 'Footpaths and Fells of Herdwick District' - and spent hours photographing and sketching and annotating all the routes in incredible detail. They are now an historical record in their own right. I'm told that second-hand copies still sell on E-bay and people still collect them. I've heard that the Herdwick Gazette is thinking of bringing out a re-print as it still receives requests for them from all over the country. They'll go well with his old office desk which they've already taken as an exhibit. Anything else?'

'Yes, there is. This.'

Lisa reached into her pocket and pulled out a small, wafer-thin plastic square with a paper label stuck to it with the word *'Lisa'* written on it.

'Err, is that an old floppy disk? I haven't seen one of those in decades. Now that is modern history. I wonder what's on it.'

'Well, I was curious myself so I managed to find someone with some ancient gear who was able to fire it up and read it. I'm not sure that the contents should be made available to the museum though.'

'Now I'm really intrigued.'

'Well, you may not remember but in 2001 I took a gap year between getting my B.A and starting my M.A. I went 'Teaching English as a Foreign Language' on mainland China for six months. At that time travel to the Peoples' Republic of China was just opening up and I was the only European living in the City of Huainan. Phone calls to and from China were difficult to make and very expensive so I exchanged e-mails with my parents instead – mostly regular short ones with my mother. In between her e-mails, about once a month, Dad would write longer ones. Initially they were intended to help me overcome my home-sickness, especially as that was when Mam was just starting with her illness although, to be fair, we didn't know then how bad that would become. As you know, working for the

Council was his life so Dad would tell me about issues that arose at work, about his colleagues at the Council and about his clashes with the Councillors. He called them 'Herdwick Tales'.'

'I guess most of the people mentioned in them will be dead by now.'

'Maybe so but they might offend the descendants of those people. You know what it's like in Shepdale – kick one and they all limp. However, they are interesting, particularly to me, and you can read the transcripts if you want to. As you know Dad had a very respectful and professional public manner when he worked for the Council but these e-mails show that private side of his character that he kept hidden. He does express some rather irreverent views on his colleagues and the workings of local government.'

'In that case I definitely want to read them,' said Farah. 'I just hope that he spoke kindly of me.'

11: CUT TO THE QUICK (2001)

Selwyn is Property Services Manager for the fictional Herdwick District Council. From January to June 2001 his daughter Lisa is temporarily working in mainland China. Communication is difficult so he stays in touch by sending her an e-mail once each month. He tells her about his work and the people he encounters during it.

***

From: dad@user.freeserve.co.uk

To: LisaXYZ@hotmail.com

Date: 8 January 2001 20:59

Subject: **Herdwick Tales**

Hello Lisa

Thanks for your e-mail. I'm sorry to hear that you are a bit homesick. It will pass in time. I know that your mother writes to you regularly but she says that I should also send you an occasional e-mail to cheer you up. I don't really do anything interesting outside of work apart from fell-walking, which you already know all about being the daughter of the 'Pilot of the Fells'. As nothing newsworthy really happens here I've decided to tell you some tales about work. Once you've read them you'll realise that working in China can only be better than working in local government in the UK. Remember, there is always someone worse off than you. In this case it's me. I hope that these cheer you up as they arrive.

Your story about being offered chickens' feet to eat at the Hotel Restaurant in Beijing on your outward journey was very amusing. It think that you should have tried eating them although I would have expected them to be 'fowl'. Sorry, the old jokes just keep slipping out. I know that you've been hearing them for most of your life but it's never stopped me repeating them and I can't change now. Who knows what culinary delicacies lie in store for you when you move to the less civilised interior of the country?

So, what happened to me today?

Work, work, work and what a bad day it was.

It had started on Friday when the Treasurer sent me a memo. It was his first response on the subject for four months. He was telling me that my bid for maintenance funding for all Herdwick District Council's properties for the next financial year, estimated at £1 million and which I had submitted last October, had not been approved at the first time of asking by the Finance Committee. I am to receive only £600,000, which is actually £200,000 less than last year, with April only eleven weeks away. 'Oh dear (actually something stronger really)', I thought.

I dwelt on this all Saturday and Sunday between bouts of housework and long periods on the internet trying to find out how to upgrade my home computer - as you do - and went back to work this morning determined to make somebody pay for spoiling my weekend.

I composed an e-mail to the Treasurer and copied it to the Chief Executive telling them that I couldn't maintain their buildings on such a measly sum, that I would have to sack one of my surveyors because we wouldn't have enough work to do, that I was sick of the Chief Exec always talking about communication and never doing it, that some of his buildings might have to close because they might become dangerous, that I wouldn't be responsible if somebody died (that's always a clincher because somebody did get seriously injured in the Leisure Centre once and they don't like to be reminded), that it might invalidate the Buildings Insurance policy and that I was going to report them all to the Councillors in a memo timed to arrive the day before the full Council meeting to approve the whole Council budget. Of course it was written very diplomatically with lots of mealy-mouthed phrasing like *'I can't guarantee that buildings won't have to close'* and *'people may be put at risk'* and *'it would be remiss of me not to update the Members'* etc. I'm not completely daft.

I then felt better because he is unlikely to sack me for speaking the truth, especially in such an apologetic manner. You only get sacked in Local Government for capital offences, such as being so incompetent as to not actually be able to hide it or being caught groping the Chairman against his wishes. Sorry, forget that, I'm getting mixed up - for being outstandingly and obviously incompetent you get promoted not sacked. However, those good feelings didn't last long.

After a while the I.T. lads, Steve and Kurt, turned up unexpectedly at my office. I say unexpectedly because they came to install some new computers onto the Council network that they'd bought last March when we had some slack in the budget. Those computers had been sitting under my desk in their original boxes and giving me sore knees for nearly twelve months, meaning that I had to grow longer arms to actually use the desk for work. They also brought three new computers that I had ordered through them. However they only had instructions from the I.T. Manager to install the original two and not the three new ones. I think the I.T. Manager was getting worried that the original two would go out of warranty without being tested so he needed to know whether they worked or not in case they needed to go back to the manufacturer. Anyway the three new computers are now sat under the desk instead of the original two so my longer arms and calloused knees cannot be dispensed with yet. Their parting remark was that they promised to return to install the three new computers 'sometime after Easter' but significantly did not say which Easter.

That took me to lunch time and still no word from the Treasurer or Chief Exec.

Lunchtime was a frustrating experience. I went to Ottakers Bookshop to browse *'The Idiot's Guide to Computers'* in their Technical Section. They have more modern books than the Library and the staff don't seem to mind if you don't buy anything after you've read it. I was looking to see how to upgrade the BIOS on my old home PC so that it will recognise the new 30-gig hard drive that I ordered through Shepdale Computer Centre but which had originated in China. I'm told that 30-gig is massive and that computers will never get any bigger than this.

What exactly is a gig in computer terms? Some kind of measurement of size but I'm not sure of what exactly? I always thought it was a performance by a pop group but what do I know? So will listening to my music with 30-gigs be like listening to 30 pop groups at once and make me go deaf? I know ... it's another Dad joke. Do you remember those early computer days with your

Sinclair ZX80 and the ZX Spectrum when we used to spend ages loading up games from cassette tapes with a cassette player? We thought then that a 48 KB memory was huge? It's bad enough now waiting for Freeserve to dial a connection to the internet. In either case I'll never get those hours of my life back.

I was studying in Ottakers because the I.T. lads told me that if I got the upgrade wrong the motherboard could blow up. Steve said that he had destroyed one at work and the only saving grace was that he'd been able to send it back under warranty hoping that if he said nothing they would just throw it in the bin and send him another - which they did; hence the I.T. Manager's admirable policy of setting up all computers just before the warranty runs out to test them. The significance of 'sometime after Easter' now becomes clearer. Anyway I digress, as Ronnie Corbett would say, and this rambling e-mail is certainly starting to resemble an R.C. story. I read all that I could in Ottakers but frustratingly the more I read on the subject the more I realised what I didn't know. Then the fear of blowing up my computer, which is now well out of warranty, started to magnify. So do I risk it or would it be less stressful to slip Steve a tenner to do it for me in his own time? A tenner is a tenner though, isn't it? I was still debating it as I went back to work.

On returning I was pleasantly surprised to find that John, one of the Building Surveyors, had arranged for the Service Engineers to fix the heating in the offices so we didn't have to freeze all afternoon as we had all morning. I did reflect on the possibility that it might be a long cold winter next year if the Chief Exec fails to get me the Maintenance Budget that I want. Still, I won't be freezing on my own because I will make damn sure that the system that serves his offices will be the last to be maintained of anybody's. Vengeance is a meal best served cold, they say. And it will be.

The afternoon was pretty standard depression after that. I got a letter from the Head of Food Safety asking me for a reference for my Group's part-time typist who had obviously applied for a full-time vacancy in his Group. She is bit of a hefty lass but looks perfectly attractive and healthy. She obsesses about eating and dieting in rotation and constantly talks about both extremes whilst producing reams of excellent typing. I worry that working in FOOD could be unhealthy for her. Won't the constant reminders of FOOD further feed her obsession? It's depressing for me because if I give her a good reference and she gets the job then I will have to go to the trouble of finding a replacement. Also the Head of FOOD will hate me if she then eats herself into a stupor, can't do the job, goes off sick and he has to pay her whilst also hiring an agency stand-in at additional cost. Or maybe I'm wrong. Might she be so influenced by typing out prohibition notices for unhygienic restaurants that it reinforces her resolve to avoid many of them at lunchtime when she is dieting? I can't decide what's for the best. Oh the life and death decisions that you have to make as a manager! I bet she'd have tackled those chickens' feet that you refused in Beijing though.

Anyway that was the end of a bad but thoroughly typical day at work. I find myself thinking more and more about early retirement on days like these.

The Treasurer and the Chief Exec have still not come back to me about the maintenance budget cuts.

E-mail me soon and let me have your impressions of life in China.

12: THE U-TURN (2001)

From: Selwyn@herdwickdc.gov.uk

To: LisaXYZ@hotmail.com

Date: 12 February 2001 17:42

Subject: **Herdwick Tales**

Dear Lisa

Thanks for your e-mail. I'm pleased that you're feeling happier and that you have settled into your new accommodation after your move to Huainan.

It's amusing to hear that you are regarded as something of a celebrity and were invited to meet the City Mayor simply because you are the only European in the province. It's even more amazing that your meeting with him was filmed for the local TV. I mean, he's the Mayor of a massive Chinese city whilst you come from a rural backwater (where the sheep outnumber the residents) and are just straight out of Uni on a gap year. At least you have your American companion to spread the load of the civic engagements that are likely to follow once word gets around that you and she are the only white people in that province. If you get the chance can you use your privileged status to ask the Mayor if he can send someone round to the local industrial estate to ask what is happening about the complaint that I made via Shepdale Computer Centre to the Chinese supplier about the destruction of my motherboard following the installation of their 30-gig hard drive into my home PC? I am now compelled to type this e-mail at work before I can go home. And yes, I did try to save that tenner by doing it myself and not paying Steve from IT to fix it for me. And yes I will learn from it (can you hear echoes of your Mam :-) in that phrase?)

Well it was a slightly better day at work today.........plotting and politics combined....but where to begin?

I suppose it all started about twelve months ago when young Lloyd Simpkin (his wealthy Dad owns the local Ferrari franchise) was elected to the Council as the Member for Lower Ayeside (or LA - like Los Angeles – as we know it), a prosperous ward out in the sticks.

With a name like Lloyd it was inevitable that he had to be a bit of a 'banker' as the cockneys would say. That's not to say that he isn't intelligent. Unfortunately he's a Tory and his stated ambition is to become Prime Minister (because he doesn't have a real job already). So it isn't hard to picture him as a William Hague clone with hair. (Hague is currently Leader of Her Majesty's Opposition with the same ambition as Lloyd although his tenure is looking shaky). Young Lloyd, although he must be older, only looks about 15 years of age. I keep wanting to ask him if his Dad knows that he's not in school. Of course, being a part-time career politician, he puts himself about a bit and gets onto every Committee and working party that he can shove his nose into, including one that I have to attend - the Affordable Housing Working Party - dealing with Council-sponsored housing developments. And being a chancer it wasn't long before he wanted to come up with an early success to make his mark in the community.

So he notices a bit of grazing land that the Council owns in LA and publicly suggests that we develop it in partnership with Two Sheds Housing Association (they have the money to build) for low cost housing for local people, not knowing that it had already been turned down for planning permission by the Council's own Planning Committee in the past. (Only a Council could refuse consent on its own land for a scheme that another part of the Council wants to use it for - it's an unreal world that I work in at the best of times.) Anyway he persists and I get the unenviable task of trying to turn his dreams into reality.

Knowing that I have little chance of getting a

straightforward consent after the first refusal I needed to come up with a new angle. So I looked to the Doctors for a cure. By co-incidence, and life is full of these little co-incidences, the local Doctor's practice is looking to expand into bigger premises and has been considering developing a new surgery on land owned by Herdwick Farmers' Cooperative next to their new supermarket. So far so good, but Herdwick Farmers' Cooperative is screwing the Doctors for an arm and a leg for the site purchase. However planning consent is not certain on that site either, although the general pressure of public opinion in LA is very much in favour of a new surgery somewhere ... anywhere. So the Doctors ask 'can we buy the Council's land instead for the surgery subject to planning consent?'

This is where I have my brilliant idea. I suggest to the Affordable Housing Working Party that we sell half of our site to the Doctor's on condition that we put in a joint planning application for the surgery on half and affordable housing on the other half. If we sell the Doctor's half to them at a reasonable price they will be happy and we get some welcome money plus housing on the other half where previously we couldn't, just by utilizing the overwhelming public pressure to get a new surgery. Simply amazing! They all go for it and Lloyd is my latest best friend and I am the hero of the hour. 'Or so I thought,' to quote from

Hugh Grant's best man speech in 'Four Weddings and a Funeral'. Things in the world of Local Government are never that simple. Anyway I draw a red line on a map to show the field boundaries and bang in a joint outline planning application with Two Sheds HA as quickly as possible. Then I sit back and wait.

After a while, the public begins to hear about it as word gets around. A groundswell of NIMBY's and anti-social housing opposition is quite normal – the 'I don't want council tenants living next door to me as it will affect the price of my house' types. One bigoted old dear actually said to me 'I don't want to live next door to Rastas with Ghetto-blasters. That's why I left London.'

However we also get opposition from the 'don't spoil my view of the historic Ayeside Bridge' brigade led by the Civic Society, from the Parish Council who don't want anything in LA to change ever and from neighbouring council tenants living in an old folks sheltered housing complex who, surprisingly because the Doctor's queues are full of them, don't want to live next door to 'drug addicts living in cheap houses who will be breaking into the surgery every night to feed their habit whilst slamming car doors when parking on the residents car park'. Can you believe it? Every nutcase in LA has crawled out of the woodwork to have a pop at us.

Not surprisingly Lloyd, and a few other Tories from the Working Party who can see hordes of voters deserting them at the next election, start to get cold feet.

The next thing is that Herdwick Farmers' Co-operative hear about it and see that the chance of them making a quick buck by selling their alternative surgery site is disappearing fast. So they bang in their planning application double quick and now we have a race, the speed of which is, quite bizarrely, being controlled by our own Planning Department who announce that they are only prepared to recommend consent for one site, but won't say which one they favour. Like all good local government officers, they want to sit on the fence and feel which way the wind is blowing up their trouser legs.

Then Herdwick Farmers' Cooperative lops a chunk off their price for the land to rival our low asking price as a gesture of goodwill to the community (i.e. their shoppers). The Doctors then change their minds and decide they like the Herdwick Farmers' Cooperative site better at the reduced price. Can it get any worse? YES! Some of the Councillors who are on the Affordable Housing Working Party, and who are supposed to want an affordable housing for locals' development on our site, are also on the Planning Committee and are looking likely to vote against it. Hero status for me is now rapidly becoming persona-non-grata status and Lloyd is no longer my best friend. But I don't like to lose.

It all reaches a head at the next Affordable Housing Working Party. Lloyd, the William Hague man-child who proposed the scheme in the first place and who, I should have mentioned, originally argued in favour of the Doctors being sold part of the site, now reveals his true political skills. In a move worthy of any future Prime Minister he does a complete U-turn. He proposes that we withdraw our planning application entirely to give Herdwick Farmers' Cooperative a clear run at their site. The boy has no shame. I argue that we should leave our application alone as it is still the Council Planning Committee which will make the final decision and there is still a chance so long as the Herdwick Farmers' Cooperative site doesn't get consent before ours. But wait, the Planning Department has deferred our application, which was submitted first, and has now scheduled them both for the same meeting. The B......s!

This throws the advantage Lloyd's way. But just as he is about to win the day the wily Working Party Chairman, Councillor Bill Blackledge, a man who is as wide as he is tall, dresses like a miner on a day out to Blackpool and represents a part of the Council District as different from snobby LA as you can get, manages to stage a late rally. He is backed by a Liberal Member who supports affordable housing as a business principle (they bring in customers to his local shop), hates Tories and sees slapping Lloyd down as good sport. They succeed in persuading the rest to amend our application so that it will go forward to the Planning meeting but only for half the site for housing alone with no Doctor's surgery included. What a move! We are still in with a chance of something. The die is cast and we are set for the final showdown at the next Planning Committee. Phew ... I breathe a sigh of temporary relief.

Unfortunately, the relief doesn't last long. At the Planning Committee the Herdwick Farmers' Cooperative application is up first and is approved without a murmur of protest. The Press and Public Gallery is packed with NIMBY's and other assorted opponents with a scattering of zimmer frames from the neighbouring Sheltered Housing scheme all out for blood. They are allowed to address the Committee and do so earnestly despite a complete absence of facts. Members are swaying but Councillor Bill pulls them back with a heart-felt plea on behalf of the homeless of Herdwick. It's going to be close. They take a vote, it's 5 - 5, but wait, Lloyd hasn't yet raised his hand ... it slowly rises from his side ... it's against! The housing scheme is lost and, unique in this Council's history, it has turned down its own planning application on its own same site for the second time. The forces of darkness have triumphed in a dramatic finale.

And so, back to today and plotting and politics. I don't like to lose, but how to win without making enemies of influential members like Lloyd? There's no point in upsetting him as he may pop up in future on the Personnel Sub-Committee and vote against my next pay rise out of spite. So a plan is formed with the help of willing Wesley, the Housing Manager, who wants the houses more than anybody because it's his responsibility to deliver these schemes to meet Government targets (i.e. his job depends on it). He also has to explain to our Housing Association partners why we lost this scheme and their planning application fees along with it.

The plan is dastardly in its cunning. The Council as a matter of policy will not appeal its own planning refusal decision. However Two Sheds Housing Association's name appears as joint applicant on the planning application so they can appeal the refusal to the Secretary of State for the Environment. The Minister's Inspector can, if he is persuaded, overrule the Council's decision and that would be final and binding on the Council. So, sod Lloyd and the Planning Committee. The way to do it is to whisper it in Councillor Bill's ear so that he can suggest it at the next Working Party meeting and take Lloyd by surprise, having done a good lobbying job on everybody else in advance. It also has the advantage of keeping me out of the firing line. Wesley has agreed to deliver the message and I look forward to sitting on the side-lines whilst Bill stokes it up all over again.

The Chief Exec still hasn't got back to me about the proposed cut in the maintenance budget. Other than that, as I said, a slightly better day today. Write soon

13: ACCOMMODATING NASA (2001)

From: dad@user.freeserve.co.uk

To: LisaXYZ@hotmail.com

Date: 12 March 2001 20:43

Subject: **Herdwick Tales**

Hello Lisa

Thanks for your e-mail.

The Chinese supplier rejected my complaint so I had to take my PC back to Shepdale Computer Centre and have a new motherboard installed at considerable expense. So I can return to emailing you from home. Your Mother has banned me from studying 'PCs for Idiots' in Ottakers bookshop at lunchtime.

I'm pleased to see that your celebrity status is continuing in China although I'm alarmed to hear that you have become a public safety hazard. I suppose it's inevitable that people will stop and stare at a tall, blond, white woman walking down the street in a land of short, dark-haired Asian people but to cause a road accident involving pedestrians, cyclists and cars in the main shopping area is taking things just a bit too far. I suggest that you wear a headscarf, dispense with heels and walk with your knees bent when out in public so that no-one notices you. Or else just go out at night.

Most of the people that I meet relate to work and a mixed and varied bunch of weirdos they are. None more so than the Councillors who I work for. The problems that I have been experiencing recently with the shortage of maintenance funding in my budget make me recall my experience with Councillor Blunt. Not that he was a weirdo. However, he had a disability problem that confined him to a wheelchair and that did cause problems.

Councillor Blunt, an ordinary and pleasant enough bloke, had won his seat on the Council at a time when the Government was altering the Ward boundaries. That meant that he could only stand for one year and then have to seek re-election in the altered Ward. Nevertheless his initial election caused us a problem because we had never had a disabled Councillor before. We have had plenty of odd-looking ones and some who were obviously lacking a full deck and even some who gave all the appearance of being dead when sat in Committee meetings but never before had we had one who went everywhere on wheels.

These were not ordinary wheels either, but high-tech, space-age wheels attached to a very nippy but large electric moon buggy. Not the bog-standard wheelchair for Councillor Blunt - oh no - he had to have something that looked like it had been built by NASA. The problem was that the Town Hall just wasn't designed for disabled access. Apparently there can't have been any disabled people in Victorian times when they built it or else they were banned by law from taking office. It's all stone steps and changing levels, tight corners and narrow toilets. In fact it must have been designed by an Architect who deliberately hated disabled people and Property Managers of the future. Anyway we couldn't get him and his moon buggy into the Council Chamber for the meetings.

He was quite reasonable about this and could see the sense in not spending a fortune just for the sake of it and for a while we relocated the meetings into another large room near the Town Hall entrance which co-incidentally had a level entry from the street and was near the Town Hall disabled toilet. You would think that that was sufficient ... but you would be wrong. The pressure from the do-gooders and the disability lobby and those Council officers responsible for things like 'the environment' and those Councillors who thought that Council meetings didn't have the same feeling of importance if not held in the Council Chamber began to build up a head of steam. They thought that the Council Chamber must be made to provide the right facilities, regardless of the fact that it was a 'listed building', meaning that we couldn't alter it much at all because of the planning regulations and that to provide everything that was needed would mean just about knocking the place down and starting again. But the pressure won out and we were instructed to find a solution.

I asked one of the Architects from Design Group to look into it. This gets me back to my budget because there was very little money in the Disability Access Fund (well it didn't crop up much as a subject - he was our first disabled Councillor after all) and so, as always happened, I had to find the money out of the Maintenance budget. Yes, that same maintenance budget that was about to be cut. So I did, and the Architect came up with a reasonably good solution ... up to a point.

The old Town Hall had a link corridor to the offices in the modern extension block at its rear and we decided that Councillor Blunt could park his car in the 3-storey staff car park behind those offices, mount his moon buggy and drive through the automatic doors into the entrance to that modern block. We moved the plumbed-in coffee machine from the entrance lobby to let him drive into the lift so that he could get out at the first floor and negotiate numerous but level passageways in the modern offices to reach the link corridor.

The link corridor had three steps up to the Town Hall and a tea trolley lift beside them. It already had an automatic door with remote push button access to allow the tea lady to get the trolley through. We converted the existing tea trolley lift into a moon buggy lift to avoid those steps to get it into the link corridor and from there he could roll to the Council Chamber entrance on a level run. On the way he could use the wider staff toilets in the modern offices where we put grab handles in the Gents to help him get in and out of one of the cubicles.

We ignored that this new route meant him taking a trip of about a hundred yards from the carpark in comparison to the use of the alternative room at the front of the Town Hall which only meant a direct drive of about five yards from the Sheepfold Lane entrance. We also played down the possibility that he might get fried to a crisp or trampled to death if a fire broke out in either building. What the hell! And so what if it cost a lump of money to achieve it. Who cares? It was only the taxpayers paying for it. A brilliant solution........except for one problem. We still couldn't get him through the narrow Council Chamber entrance from the link corridor because of the combination of a tight 180 degree U-turn and outward opening fire doors.

So we did all the preliminary works to get him to that point anyway and then sent for the Fire Officer and the Planning Officer to seek advice on how to overcome the last hurdle. One suggestion was to give the caretakers a mobile phone so that he could ring them in advance and book an appointment to be carried into the Council Chamber. The flaw in this was obvious. One bad back and the caretakers' eyes would be lighting up like cash tills at the thought of the injury compensation. Another solution was to provide a transfer vehicle like a sedan chair or a wheelchair but again the lifting element was too risky and god help us if they dropped him. We would have had two claims then.

All this took twelve months to resolve and whilst we were waiting they held the next election and he was voted off the Council by the electorate. So that solved the problem of the last obstacle because we never did come up with a solution.

And, finally. The Chief Exec got back to me today about the proposed maintenance budget. He says that I'll have to live with the cut and should draw up a list of properties to sell to relieve the maintenance burden. (The man is so crazy that he'll be wanting to close all the public conveniences next – as if that will ever happen.) Thereafter he'll be carrying out a review of the staffing in my Group because we'll have less properties to maintain. I sense an early retirement opportunity.

In your next e-mail you must let me know how you get on at the civic dance. I never realised that ballroom dancing was such a popular pastime in China. Hopefully the collisions on the dance floor will be less severe than the traffic accidents in the main street even if everyone is looking at you as they waltz past.

Write soon.

14: BUTTING HEADS (2001)

From: dad@user.freeserve.co.uk

To: LisaXYZ@hotmail.com

Date: 2 April 2001 20:42

Subject: **Herdwick Tales**

Hello Lisa

Your six months in China are already more than half over. How time flies. Your Mother tells me that you need a favour but that, for a change, you are giving me plenty of warning. Can you confirm if she has got this right please? She says that you regularly lecture to a class of 40 students and that it's customary for the teacher to give each student a small gift to remember them by when the teacher leaves. She says that you require 40 picture postcards of Herdwick district scenes, all different if possible, one for each student. At least you have given me plenty of warning to scour the tourist gift shops of Shepdale over lunchtimes (though it may interfere with my browsing in Ottakers bookshop or my sampling the delights of the Wandering Tup) and allowed long enough for them to be sent in bulk by parcel post to China in time for you to hand them out.

You do realise that most scenes of Herdwick district will include photos of sheep and that all Herdwicks look alike. You might have to explain to your students that they are not photos of how the local population has evolved over centuries of walking the fells – but then again!

Speaking of Herdwicks, I had to carry out an inspection of a field full of them last week. I like to keep my hand in with some real work occasionally just as a change from all my management responsibilities – like monitoring budgets and deciding who can book two weeks leave in August to avoid everyone taking the same two weeks off. Fortunately the weather was fine when I went to inspect the field.

The Council lets various parcels of land on 360 day mowing and grazing licences to local farmers. The letting periods all end in March each year and the licences carry no protection for the users under the Agriculture Acts so they have to remove their stock by the end of the 360 day period. Offering them to let again by tender is a lot of work for relatively small annual increases in income and they are often won by the same farmers every year so in recent years we've tended to offer them back to the existing user first at modest increases to save on tendering and advertising costs.

Farmer Spelk enjoys 60 acres of the Council's

rough pasture and enclosed fell adjoining his farm east of Winander. He is known to be a difficult customer who has resisted rent increases in the past so I decided on a new approach this year. I arranged to meet him at the land to walk its boundaries and check the fences that he is liable to maintain under the licence. He was expecting me to offer it to him again at the existing rent but I wanted an increase. When he arrived I reminded him to get his stock off the land that day and told him that I wanted to walk all the boundaries and check for faults in any fences and dry-stone walls and take a photographic record. Most licensees try to ignore repairs and just stick sheep-netting or corrugated metal sheets into the gaps as the walls collapse for as long as they can get away with it. Usually we are too busy to inspect properly and they do get away with it so the gaps mount up.

I knew that he limped badly from being butted on the knee by an aggressive ram as a young man. He used to bring his fleeces in for baling to the Herdwick Farmers' Cooperative depot where I worked for a couple of summers, years ago when I was in the sixth form. Someone had told me about his misfortune then. Some details stick with you and there's no substitute for local knowledge. Farmer Spelk relied heavily on his collies to do the leg-work for him but even the most intelligent of collies isn't capable of agreeing boundary defects with me. He groaned but reluctantly decided to come with me. I opened the boot of my car to reach for my wellies, dramatically revealing to him some laminated 'To Let by Tender' posters, with tie-strings already attached, just lying there, face up, ready for attaching to the field gates.

'Ar' yon signs fer 'ere?' he asked.

'They are if we can't agree a sensible rent increase by the time I get back to the car,' I said.

'An' yer wants me to lowp rown yon walls now, wi' mi gammy leg?'

'Yes.'

'An' yer wants mi to pay fer fixin' t'gaps in 'em?'

'Yes, but if the rent's good enough we could postpone that for another year.'

We hadn't got a third of the way round before he was having a hard time keeping up with me. We reached a deal fairly quickly on a higher rent and agreed to abandon the boundary inspection until next year when his son could do it, and in the meantime he offered to do some stone repairs himself as it would be cheaper. As with Herdwicks, there has to be a winner in every head-butting contest.

That reminds me of a recent tale of two other

ornery rams butting heads that might amuse you. It can be entertaining at Council meetings because of the characters involved and it does get pretty heated on occasion. I mentioned the affordable housing site in LA in a previous e-mail. Councillor Bill Blackledge raised the possibility of Two Sheds Housing Association appealing the planning application refusal at the recent Affordable Housing Working Party and completely wrong-footed young Councillor Lloyd Simpkin. The meeting was lively enough but the stand-up scuffle in the Town Hall corridor afterwards was truly something to commit to memory. Lloyd was not happy about Bill's politicking. Nothing really happened except for a bit of pushing and shoving and a few raised voices but by the time the tale circulated around the Council offices it was as if war had broken out. There had to be a conduct inquiry. Little came of it in the end but I was told of one classic outburst to the conduct panel from Bill. When spouting forth about the charges being investigated Bill launched into a monologue stating that he did not agree with what was being alleged against him and ended with "and I know who the ***alligators*** are." Much mirth in the Council Chamber.

Councillor Bill Blackledge is quite wide for his height. He is built like one of those toys that you see in the bottom of a budgie cage which rolls upright every time you knock it over. I couldn't see young Lloyd knocking him over even if he'd landed a good punch and, if he had, he would have just bounced upright again. We have some other Councillors who are even more portly than Bill. Councillors Milk and Milk are a married couple representing adjoining wards on the edge of the district. They are both pretty large people, thus being nicknamed 'Full-fat' and 'Double cream'. Neither of them drives a car so in recent years Bill, who has to pass through their area, has taken to bringing them in to Council meetings in his Land Rover. I was at a recent Committee meeting when Bill raised the question of Councillor's travelling expenses. When asked by the Chief Executive 'What's the issue?' he stated that he wasn't happy with the current mileage-based rate for using his car. He suggested that he should be switched onto a weight-based allowance if he was to continue delivering the Milk. More mirth and merriment from the spectators.

You will know by my constant references to it that I have been waiting to hear about next year's Maintenance Budget. Well the Chief Exec got back to me first thing this morning with a final decision after a very late March Full Council meeting. It seems that my prompting and lobbying and diplomatic warnings have had some measure of success. I didn't get the £1 million that I asked for but I did get the same as last year - £800,000. The Treasurer is finding the extra £200,000 over the threatened cut to £600,000 from reserves. It still represents a cut in real terms when inflation is taken into account but it is better than I expected in January. It also means that I don't have to make a Building Surveyor redundant. However it may also mean that the threatened review is postponed, which is good in one way but bad in that my chances of early retirement on enhanced terms may be rapidly disappearing. So mixed feelings about that.

Remember me mentioning my hefty part-time typist with the food obsession who applied for the full-time post in the FOOD Safety Group? She worked her notice last week and left a big gap in all our lives (no pun intended) which I've had to fill with agency staff. We took her out for a meal at lunchtime on her last day and we haven't seen her since. She may still be at the restaurant for all I know, working her way through the menu. I'd applied to recruit a permanent replacement but got a reply from HR today with bad news. As soon as Steve and Kurt from IT have installed the new computers there will be a standard Word Processing program available on the Council's Intranet with model layouts for letters, memos and reports for all staff to do their own typing. Training will be provided for everyone except for the Chief Executive who has exempted himself and will retain his voluptuous secretary on the grounds that she also provides services to the Chairman of the Council. How very convenient.

All existing typists including my ex-colleague will be subject to an appraisal to determine if they can be redeployed into any existing Council vacancies. Maybe she can become a Technical Assistant in FOOD and combine health inspections with her passion for eating and dieting. Is this another Industrial Revolution in Herdwick district? Will the rise of IT resulting in the loss of typists replicate what happened in the textile industry when industrialisation attracted all the cottage wool-knitters to the big cities to retrain as cotton spinners and weavers resulting in the bottom falling out of the Herdwick underpants monopoly overnight? It took us years to pull our socks up and develop new products. What we need is some young inventor to find a new use for Herdwick wool. It might happen in your life-time Lisa but probably not in mine.

Jim, the Senior Committee Clerk, tells me that the Tourism Committee had a one-item urgent meeting today at the written request of a Ward Member. It seems that Councillors are worried that following the opening of the Eden Project in Cornwall on 17 March, tourism numbers coming to Herdwick (at the opposite end of the country – I ask you) are expected to dip dramatically. To counteract the £37.5 million grant made to the Eden Project by the Lottery Commission the Tourism Committee decided to make a grant of £2000 for increased advertising to the Herdwick Visitor Centre and Guesthouse up in the Shepdale Valley. Yes, that will certainly give the Eden Project something to think about and will no doubt secure the sitting Councillor's seat for that Ward in the upcoming local elections. One has to spend to compete in the international world of tourism and politics. As a Council-tax payer I think that they have invested my money wisely and I will sleep soundly tonight :-). At least they didn't decide to waste it on fees just for a consultant to tell them that better advertising might help.

Postcard purchasing for your students will begin in earnest as soon as you confirm that I've fully understood your requirements.

Write soon.

15: PILOT OF THE FELLS (2001)

A PICTORIAL GUIDE FOR WALKERS
BY
SELWYN (THE PILOT OF THE FELLS)

FOOTPATHS AND FELLS
OF
HERDWICK DISTRICT

VOLUME ONE

PRINTED BY THE HERDWICK GAZETTE

From: dad@user.freeserve.co.uk

To: LisaXYZ@hotmail.com

Date: 16 May 2001 20:22

Subject: **Herdwick Tales**

Hello Lisa

How are you getting on with the language barrier in China? I know that all your students are learning English from you and presumably they have some existing understanding as I'm aware that you do not speak Mandarin. Presumably you have an interpreter assigned to you? There's not much call for other languages in Herdwick district apart from in the summer when the Japanese tourists arrive. They come to experience the Walter Winster Town Trail and to see his exhibition in Shepdale Museum and to enjoy the Herdwick Visitor Experience up the Shepdale Valley. Who would have thought that a Herdwick dialect poet would have achieved such a following from as far away as Japan and such a long time after his death? It's something to do with his writing being the inspiration for the 'Save the Planet' movement.

I did pick up a few phrases of Japanese from that 1980s TV series 'Shogun'. Is Chinese anything like Japanese? They live in roughly the same part of the world so you'd think that they'd have some commonality of language. But I suppose it's probably as similar as VHS was to Betamax. Oh sorry, you probably don't know what Betamax was. Take it from me that they were the same but also very different.

Anyway 'Shogun' was a brilliant series and I was really pleased when you bought me that VHS cassette one Christmas so I could view it again (and again and again). Richard Chamberlain, an American actor played Blackthorne, the pilot of the first English ship to reach Japan in the 17th century. I could understand what he was saying as his Japanese was delivered with a western accent. So phrases like ...

'Wakaremasu' (I understand),

'Konnichi wa' (How are you?),

'Hai' (yes),

'Sayonara' (Goodbye) and

'Nane mo' (It's nothing)

... were easy to comprehend. However the only phrase that I could understand spoken by the Japanese actors, because of their rapid speech and accent, was ...

'Domo anjin-san' (thanks Mr Pilot).

'Pilot' resonated with me because of the nick-name 'Pilot of the Fells' that the Herdwick Gazette had applied to me when they'd published my fell-walking guides. However I can't see the Japanese word for 'pilot' being much use to me in the streets of Shepdale or even if I ever visit Japan. I certainly wouldn't want to recognise it if I'm flying to Tokyo and the stewardess rushes down the aisle of the plane shouting some Japanese phrase that includes the word *'anjin'*. That might be worrying.

Jim, the Senior Committee Clerk and Eric from Finance and I were having a lunchtime pint in the Tup sometime last summer, as we do very occasionally :-). There was a party of Japanese tourists also having lunch, after first checking out the historic spot on the pavement outside the pub where Walter Winster had met his untimely death. One of them asked me, in perfect English, for directions to the museum. I told him how to find it and really hoped that he'd thank me for my helpful directions with *'Domo anjin-san'* so that I could impress him with *'Nane mo'* and flabbergast Jim and Eric with my language skills. However the Japanese guy just said 'Thanks' in English and wandered off before I could even bring my phrase to mind.

Now I practice my phrases at work so I'll be ready next time. The Principal Engineer from the Architecture and Design Group has grown a small goatee beard and looks just like that Japanese actor that plays Mr Miyagi in 'The Karate Kid' film. Whenever I visit his office I put my hands together and bow and say *'Konnichiwa, Miyagi-san'*. He rolls his eyes and moves his hands in circles as if showing the Kid how to clean his car and then gives me his variation on Mr Miyagi's famous line 'Wax on, wax off', except that his is 'Wax on, p*** off'. That requires no translation.

Perhaps those phrases aren't much use to you in China so I won't mail the VHS cassette to you. Maybe you should try watching Chinese TV instead whilst you're over there. You might pick up a few useful phrases. Just a suggestion – please feel free to ignore it.

I had a really good day today but managed to cause a bit of a panic in the office. After a recent Health and Safety initiative I'd had a whiteboard fixed to the wall by the main office door. Then I'd told all the Property Services staff that they had to write all destinations and expected return times against their initials on the board each time that they went out on site so that those in the office could check on them if they didn't return on time; just in case they were lying dead or injured somewhere on site. Well would you believe it, being a brand new system, I totally forgot to log my own movements on it today? So no-one knew where I was for all of the morning.

I'd gone to one of my favourite places; the basement under Shepdale Town Hall. It's a wonderful place. It's warm from the heat of the boilers and quiet with no windows and no telephones. The Council's Leases and Deeds are stored there in one room behind a steel vault door. Another room has my historic Estates files stored on timber racks. Those files are like my children. I gave life to many of them and helped them grow into maturity before waving them off to the store like teenagers going off to university. I can't get the same feeling about copies of my letters being held in the computer, even if I could get Steve and Kurt from IT to install the new PCs – Easter has been and gone and I'm still waiting.

Other Groups also have store rooms in the basement but staff rarely visit so there's no-one to bother you. I just love it down there in that underground world. Old Arthur, the guy that trained me as a surveyor when I was a youth, introduced me to its magic. Once in 1973 we spent weeks down there splitting up the old Shepdale Municipal Borough Council Deeds between the new County and District responsibilities ready for Local Government Reorganisation. It has an old map table for spreading out large documents and a battered leather Chesterfield armchair that I can sit in to read them. It's far quicker to go there myself than wait weeks for the Solicitors to answer questions about property titles. They got so fed up of me moaning at them about delay in the days when I worked for Shepdale MBC that they gave me the spare key to their vault door. I just wish that Steve and Kurt could have downloaded Arthur's memory onto a hard drive before he retired. He really knew his way around the basement contents. One day I hope that Farah will say the same about me.

The only problem is that the warmth and quiet in the basement does tend to make me want to nod off, which I did for an hour just before lunchtime. I don't feel guilty as the Council owes me many hours of unclaimed flexi-time which I write-off every month. However the staff expressed concern about my unrecorded absence on the whiteboard when I got back. I just told them the truth. That I couldn't remember anything from walking from my office towards the whiteboard this morning on my way out until my recent return just before lunchtime, so 'I must have been abducted by aliens'.

I was in the basement for two reasons. The first related to a case where I will have to give evidence in Lanchester County Court. A couple of years ago there was an accident outside the public toilets in Winander town centre. A woman tripped over the edge of a manhole and broke her hip. She is claiming compensation for damages. The Council's Insurers want to defend against the claim. I have to give evidence as Property Manager about my Group's regular recorded maintenance inspection regime to say that we knew about the manhole, had it on a list of items to check and had ticked it as not defective and in need of repair. Of course we have no such formal recorded maintenance inspection regime. The Building Surveyors just go and look every month and issue Works Orders for repairs that they notice on that visit rather than record items that don't need fixing. When nothing needs doing there is no written evidence of any visit. So I was in the Treasurer's store room in the basement trying to find copies of old Travelling Expense claim forms as evidence of how regularly my Building Surveyors visited the premises before and after the accident. Who will compensate me for the nosebleed that I will likely have to endure brought on by travelling over the District boundary to visit Lanchester for a battering from a fancy Barrister?

My second reason was to research a Deed relating to some open space land on the top side of Shepdale. A developer wants to widen an access over that land via an existing narrow trackway to build houses on his land below the Council's open space land. I marvel at those old copperplate handwritten Deeds – land colourwashed pink owned by the Council, rights of way coloured brown, land benefitting from the rights coloured blue, all preserved forever on linen. The sale prices are in pounds, shillings and pence. Linear measurements are recorded in yards and feet. Areas are in acres, square yards and square feet. Some are in roods and perches. The youngsters like Farah struggle with those imperial concepts but it's the world of my early training before metrication, where I am king of all I survey.

I checked the width of the track coloured brown on plan with the 6-inch wooden imperial scale ruler that has lived in my inside jacket pocket for the last three decades. I smiled when I confirmed that the track coloured brown on plan was nowhere near wide enough to accommodate a standard housing estate road or permit visibility splays at its exit and looked forward to extracting a ransom from the developer under the Stokes v Cambridge ruling. We haven't had one of those jobs for a while and Farah will enjoy the negotiation once we've got her a metric plan to work from.

The day just got better and better. I left the office after lunch, having noted my intentions on the whiteboard – I couldn't use the aliens' justification twice in one day or it might undermine my credibility - and went for a pint and a mutton pie with Jim and Eric in the Tup. After lunch I strolled up town in glorious sunshine to inspect the open space, measure the access width, take a photograph of it and enjoy the spectacular view across Shepdale's rooftops to the distant hills whilst I planned my next fell-walk in my head. On days like these I think that I should pay the Council to let me work there. It really doesn't get any better.

Do you recall me mentioning the fight between the two Councillors in the corridor of Shepdale Town Hall in my last e-mail? It's started a political trend. All this evening's TV news headlines feature John Prescott, the Deputy Prime Minister, punching a protester who threw an egg at him in Rhyl. Where Herdwick leads the world follows. At least JP connected with his swing. It could signal the end of democracy as we know it but the entertainment factor would increase dramatically.

The only cloud on my horizon is the need to take your Mam to the hospital for some tests next week. She will tell you all about it in her e-mail. She doesn't seem unduly worried and there's nothing you can do to help. Try not to worry about her. We'll all just have to wait for the results. She'll let you know more when we know more ourselves.

Write soon.

16: SYNERGY AND PIMPLES (2001)

From: dad@user.freeserve.co.uk

To: LisaXYZ@hotmail.com

Date: 12 June 2001 20:57

Subject: **Herdwick Tales**

Hello Lisa

Not long left to go now until your Chinese adventure ends. Your mother says that you might extend your trip by travelling across China to view the Terracotta Army before spending a bit of time in Hong Kong on the way back to England. Well why not if you can afford it? It's on the doorstep and you may never be this close to it again. Don't worry about your Mam. At least the tests showed what was wrong with her. The Doctors, whilst they never give any guarantees, say that they are optimistic about the outcome. I'll book some leave from work to look after her for when she comes out and for later when she has the chemo. I may as well use up my holidays for that as she won't be fit enough to go away this summer and you might as well take advantage of that before you go back to Uni. She doesn't want you rushing home as there's nothing that you can do to change things.

I'm pleased that the box of scenic Herdwick postcards arrived ready for you give out to each of your students as a farewell gift. Presumably you are building a complete English lesson around explaining the concept of postcards. I was a bit worried that the box might have been impounded by Chinese customs as a suspicious package. I mean, who else other than British wool-smugglers attempting to drum up new clients would send pictures of Herdwick sheep halfway around the world?

How are you getting on with putting personal notes on all forty of them? Hopefully you are writing them in English not Mandarin. It must make it much easier for you with each student having adopted an English name. I'm amused and impressed by their choices. Young mothers aren't naming their babies Gladys, Ethel and Winifred over here anymore. Now we have little Beyonces, Pinks and Madonnas. Madonna ... what's all that about? At least the names Gladys, Ethel and Winifred fit with the Chinese craze for ballroom dancing. Maybe they'll switch names to Madonna, Beyonce etc when they catch up with our songs. You never said, did your feet survive your night at the last ball?

Steve and Kurt from IT Group came round today to install the new computers previously stored under my desk. You may remember me mentioning them in my first e-mail last January when they were delivered. Only 5 months waiting this time. Things are improving. Why do boffins always travel in pairs? Is it for protection against the abuse that they deserve for never coming when you want them to? Anyway, they did the job and everyone in my Group is now connected to the Internet and the Intranet. Don't ask me what the difference is because I couldn't understand Kurt when he tried to explain it. Something about one being connected outside the Council and one only being inside the Council but both doing similar things. A bit like the good old days with VHS and Betamax digital recorders then, eh? Nobody knew that difference either. Oh sorry, I forgot you still have no idea what Betamax is … or was :-). Just put it down to your youth.

This morning the Chief Exec called in all Group Managers for a presentation in the Council Chamber in Shepdale Town Hall. I thought that he had forgotten about reviewing my Group after the Maintenance budget was restored in March. Instead he wants to review the whole Council structure (again). He said something about 'synergy' (I had to look it up) and the ability of Professional Groups to cross boundaries. For example Planners might be able to do some elements of Estates work and Architects might be able to do some elements of Public Health inspections when the pressure is on or when staff shortages arise. It's something to do with moving staff around to even out the peaks and troughs in workloads and keep the salary bill down. Apparently it needs consultants to do a Job Evaluation exercise first to find out what people do. (He's the Chief Exec, doesn't he already know what Council staff do?) It will enable him to weed out the surpluses in staffing and even-out disparities in pay. Then staff may be moved around as necessary. There could be 'winners and losers' but he expects that most staff will remain as they are at the end of it (in which case why do it at all?)

The man is as daft as a brush. Unfortunately he is not alone. What do Planners know about Estates work? They can't even do their own job properly. They just make it up as they go along. It's a fictitious profession justified by lots of fancy words with principles that change like the seasons applied by people who bend to the wind whenever anyone challenges them. They exist only to prevent constructive things happening or to justify things that should never be allowed. If I was running the country I'd do away with the Planning System. Take that convoluted fiasco about that affordable-housing-and-Doctors'-surgery application in Little Ayeside that ended with Councillors Blackledge and Simpkin scrapping in Shepdale Town Hall corridor. What a lengthy waste of time and money that was. People could still submit planning applications but under my new system the Chief Exec would just turn up in the Council Chamber each Wednesday clutching that week's bundle and decide them on the toss of a coin. Heads approved, Tails rejected. No appeals. We'd only need one Committee Clerk to record the result and one neutral witness to ensure no cheating. Get rid of all Planning Officers and the entire Planning Committee as well. Quick, cheap and no worse an outcome than the present system. That's synergy for you ... and there would be plenty of winners and losers.

And fancy employing Consultants who will no doubt charge a pretty penny to do the Job Evaluation part, probably at the expense of existing Group budgets like my maintenance funds, whilst using us to tell them everything they didn't know but should have done before they arrived. So heed my words. When you finish your MA, and should you decide on Local Government as a career choice, be warned. Old Arthur (who trained me) and I are a dying breed. Well Arthur's already dead but you know what I mean – experienced specialists who knew their jobs and stayed with one authority for life out of loyalty because they felt valued. That era is over. Youngsters like you and Farah will be endlessly reviewed and restructured in and out of work for the whole of your careers because 'change for change' sake is the new mantra. Good luck to you.

There, I feel a little better for that rant. Please

don't quote what I've just said outside of China.

We all met the Chief Exec's presentation with a stunned silence and filed out shaking our heads. How come the Chief Exec and the Directors are always exempted from these reviews?

On the way out the Chief Exec collared me. He's been talking to the CE of Lanchester City Council at a recent SOLACE (Society of Local Authority Chief Executives) meeting. LCC is buying something called PIMPLES (**P**roperty **In**formation, **M**aintenance **P**rogramme, **L**eases and **E**states **S**ystem). He says it is a software database designed to hold and sort all our property records, deeds, sales, leases, rent reviews, maintenance and servicing budgets, works orders and building running costs including energy costs. (He'd had to pause for breath at the end of that sentence. I wasn't aware that he knew that we did all those things.) He said that it will revolutionise property management in Herdwick DC and get rid of all our paper records. Apparently if we buy it in partnership with LCC we will get a big discount from the supplier and it will make the Property Services Group super-efficient. He wants me to go down to Lanchester to see a joint demo and write a report on it. I'll need some solace after that trip and no doubt my pimples will need squeezing too.

Jim, the Senior Committee Clerk, and I decided

that we deserved a pint at lunchtime as we had a lot to talk about so we went to the Tup for a change :-). A pint of Rampant Ram had never tasted better. And guess who we met there – yes, Eric from Finance. It's good to know that some things remain constant in this turbulent world.

We talked about 'synergy'. Eric isn't a Group Manager like Jim and I so hadn't been at the presentation. We gave him a summary. Then he amused us with a joke. 'What's the opposite of synergy? Answer – s'outergy.' I didn't know that accountants had a sense of humour. I still don't. And yes, it does require some explanation. According to Eric those who embrace synergy will remain *in* the Council and those that don't will be *out* on their ear. It fitted the mood – not funny at all.

In the afternoon I called my Group together and gave them a briefing on the Chief Exec's two proposed initiatives. Synergy/Job Evaluation was met with absolutely no enthusiasm from the staff. PIMPLES generated more interest, especially from the younger staff, like Farah, one of my Estates Surveyors. I predicted that computers would never get any bigger and that they would never be able to replace our jobs. Someone reminded me that's exactly what I said before the typists disappeared. I said, "Don't be rash ... I can't see the Chief Exec getting PIMPLES..." (Maybe I could have phrased that better.) How could an electronic box and a little screen hold all our enormous linen maps and 3-inch thick paper files from the past and the future? I feared that it would mean no more trips to the Town Hall basement for information. That would make old Arthur turn in his grave. I continued "...and Steve and Kurt from IT can't cope now with the Int**er**net and the Int**ra**net so how can they cope with PIMPLES too?" (My comments were getting increasingly surreal). Is Int**ra**net the opposite of Int**er**net like s'outergy is the opposite of synergy? They all sound like joke words to me.

Farah disagreed as she is a big advocate of the 'paperless office' and explained that we were on the cusp of a digital revolution. There may be more work initially to set PIMPLES up and transfer all our records into it but after that we might all obtain great benefits from it. The discussion broke up after that when one of the Building Surveyors asked how come the Chief Exec could afford to pay Consultants for his Job Evaluation exercise and could afford to consider buying this new database that we didn't need when we couldn't even get a full budget to maintain the buildings. I gave them my best answer. 'I have no idea.' They all went back to work muttering. It wasn't my finest hour as a leader but my philosophy remains firmly rooted in the Alex Ferguson school of management – we are united because everybody else is against us. In case you haven't heard about it in China, United have just won the FA Premier League title for the third season in succession, and the seventh time in nine seasons. If only our Chief Exec was as good a manager as Fergie.

After a day like that I have decided that it is definitely time for me to seek early retirement. I just need a plan. I feel certain that an opportunity will present itself in the next twelve months or so if I keep my wits about me.

Please let me know your flight details from Hong Kong so that I can arrange to drive down and collect you from the airport. I could do with a day off.

(Synergy is the interaction or cooperation of two or more organisations, substances, or other agents to produce a combined effect greater than the sum of their separate effects.)

17: THE INSURANCE POLICY (2036)

A return to 2036 to continue the conversation between Lisa and Farah in the Wandering Tup concerning the proposed exhibition to honour Selwyn following his death.

***

The wording on the electronic timeline across the front of Shepdale Town Hall's first floor balcony continued to circulate on its loop:

13:29 Friday 24 October 2036*: ... Breaking News ... Shepdale Museum honours well-known local character...*

'So, can you arrange for someone to deliver Dad's items to the museum for his exhibition or should I take them down there? Who should I ask for when I get there?'

Lisa, Selwyn's daughter from his first marriage, and Farah, the current Chief Executive of Herdwick District Council, were still seated in the window booth of the Wandering Tup looking across at the Town Hall. Lisa gathered Selwyn's museum exhibits from off the table and placed them into his old briefcase.

'Those e-mails brought back many happy memories of when I was in Property Services. I'll take the exhibits back to my office and get them delivered for you. Thanks for bringing them in,' said Farah.

'And we'll keep his e-mails a secret?'

'I think so, don't you? They're very amusing but you may be right about not wanting to upset any living descendants of some of the people mentioned in them. I'm glad that I came out of them unscathed.'

Lisa replaced the e-mail transcripts in her bag-for-life that leant against the booth's table leg.

'I wouldn't have let you read them if there'd been any unfavourable comments about you, Farah. But you knew there wouldn't be. Dad thought the world of you and he was really pleased and proud when you were promoted to Property Services Manager.'

'I thought the world of him too. He gave me a job when I started out – when being a female surveyor was still relatively rare and being a Muslim surveyor was even rarer. I'll always be grateful to him. And from then on he trained me well and gave me good advice both when he was working and after he retired. He was a great bloke.'

'He was a great Dad too. But there is one thing that bothers me about that. I found something else in that briefcase too. Something that I haven't shown you yet that puzzles me. I'd like to ask you about it if you don't mind.'

'Fire away.'

Lisa reached down to the bag and pulled out a faded brown A4 envelope marked 'Private and Confidential'.

'Dad had two very happy marriages so I can't imagine that he was interested in pornography. These seem to be rather candid photographs of people that I don't know. The photos are dated in 2001. I've no idea what they were doing in the briefcase but I thought that they must relate to his work as they were in with all his old surveying stuff. Have you any ideas? Don't wave them about as they are quite personal.'

Farah slipped the photos out of the envelope, held them close to her chest and leafed through them carefully. Then she started to laugh.

'Well, well, well. The wily old fox. I've honestly never seen these before in my life but this is so typical of Selwyn.'

'What, keeping pornographic photos?'

'No, not that at all. Do you fancy a coffee in my office? If we go back there now I can show you something that you should immediately recognise whilst I check out some facts with a quick phone call. Then I think that I can throw some light on exactly what these are.'

***

'Right, let me quickly make that phone call to check first.'

Farah closed the door and walked around her desk to sit with her back to the windows that filled the whole of the wall on that side of the room. Lisa sat opposite her. They were in the Chief Executive's office on the first floor of the new extension block built behind Shepdale Town Hall on the opposite side from Sheepfold Lane and the Wandering Tup pub. The extension block was a modern concrete and glass structure not really in keeping with the historic, limestone Town Hall. Through the full height rear glass windows Lisa could look out and down onto the open top deck of an equally modern concrete three-storey car park that now covered the old Town Hall yard. The car park utilised the slope of the hill to accommodate its decks as the gradient ran down towards the River Shep at the bottom of the glacial valley in which the town of Shepdale was situated. The view of the symmetrical limestone arches of the Shep Bridge and above it the castle ruins, perched on a mound, with the backdrop of fells rising behind the buildings on the opposite side of the river, was a typically attractive town view. It was part of what made the tourists come back year on year. Lisa had visited her father at work occasionally as a child but had never seen the particular view from inside this room.

'John? It's Farah. Remind me - were you with the Council in 2001? Good man. Can you do something for me please? You remember that old property management database that we had in Property Services Group. PIMPLES it was called. It never really worked that well did it? We spent years scanning historic information and typing data into it. Yes, that's right, the one that we bought jointly with Lanchester. Tell me please, was all that historic data digitally re-transferred into your current property management system when we replaced PIMPLES? It was? Good. Can you run a search for me quickly if I tell you what I want and then ring me back with the answer?'

Farah explained what she wanted and said goodbye.

'I could have done it myself once-over on the Intranet but I'm out of practice now and it would take me forever. John is one of the Building Surveyors in Property Services and he can do it much quicker just so long as the info is in there. Now let's have that coffee whilst we wait.'

Farah walked across the room, poured two coffees and brought them back to the desk. It was a large, solid-oak, leather-topped desk, much larger than a modern desk. It looked antique and didn't really go with the concrete and glass office or the modern chairs next to it. It had obviously been moved from the former Town Clerk's old office in the Town Hall when the new extension had been built.

'Do you recognise this desk?' Farah asked.

'I've never seen it before.'

Farah's phone rang and she held it up to her ear.

'Thanks John. That's excellent. Exactly what I thought. Same time as the floodlighting? What number? I owe you one … what?' She laughed. 'No, I don't mind you asking. But I was thinking more along the lines of a pint of Rampant Ram in the Tup next time I see you there rather than a pay rise. Nice try though. Got to go, got someone with me. Thanks again.'

She looked at Lisa and said, 'Just what I thought. Now back to this desk. Would you like to walk around this side?'

Lisa walked around the desk and stood next to Farah.

'Now back off towards the window'.

Lisa backed off.

'Do you recognise it now from that angle?'

'Yes, it's quite distinctive. So how ...?'

'That's what I was checking with John. There are 360 degree remote-controlled CCTV cameras mounted on poles around the car park. John tells me that the original system was installed along with the floodlighting in 2002. It's elderly now but he says that it was quite state-of-the-art in its day, with zoom magnification. Camera number 3 is sited right outside this window. We'd had vandals and skateboarders causing problems on the car park at night because the top deck is open. That's why we got them installed. I remember being in the Town Hall Reception once, donkeys' years ago, when Councillor Lloyd Simpkin - he's mentioned in your Dad's e-mails - was making a big fuss because someone had scratched his Ferrari. No-one can see directly into these first floor offices from the car park, even at night with the lights full on, because the top deck of the car park is at a much lower level. But, if you look out of my window you can see a camera mounted on a pole that's just at the right height to see into here. That's camera 3. Normally it points the other way onto the car park but my guess is that when it was being tested it could have been swivelled to point in any direction.'

'So the photos were stills printed from CCTV.'

'Yes. If you look at the photos again, they have a tiny information line printed across the bottom. It has the camera number - C3 in this case - followed by a date that fits in with the installation period. It also shows the time as late evening, significantly after the cleaners usually leave. That date is later in the same year than when the controversy about the alleged undemocratic vote took place, when Councillor Cedric Symons died in the Council Chamber.'

'So what has a woman straddling a naked man across this desk, obviously having sex after working hours, got to do with my Dad?'

Farah laughed. 'Well, it's not pornography; it's just real life. This is Selwyn's insurance policy.'

'Insurance for what?'

'For his early retirement. Just let me look at that last e-mail again.'

Lisa still looked puzzled but pulled them out of her bag.

Farah read out Selwyn's words from his last e-mail.

'After a day like that I've decided that it's definitely time for me to seek early retirement. I just need a plan. I feel certain that an opportunity will present

itself in the next twelve months or so if I keep my wits about me.'

Farah continued, 'It could be that he suspected what was going on in this office at night and deliberately set it up for the installer to test the cameras. Maybe one of the cleaners had noticed something and mentioned it to him. Was he hinting at it in one of his e-mails when he mentioned the Chief Exec's *'voluptuous secretary'* and that she *'provides services for the Chairman'*? They might have been at it for months before Selwyn found out. But it would have been hard to keep something like that quiet in a Council that leaks like a sieve. Quite possibly no-one knew and it was just a fortunate coincidence that fell into his lap. We'll never know. Either way, Property Services Group was managing the CCTV installation contract. I bet the Contractor was testing the system, reviewed the night footage, saw the action and brought the recording to Selwyn to show that it worked. They probably had a laugh about it too. Selwyn obviously kept it to himself. He may have asked the contractor to keep it under his hat. An outside contractor would probably want to keep Selwyn happy in the hope of further work and probably wouldn't mention it to anyone else in the Council as he likely wouldn't know the participants. This was Selwyn's opportunity.'

'For what?'

'Let me start back at the beginning. Your Mam was ill for a long time. After the first treatment the cancer came back again. Your Dad was looking for early retirement and wanted a way out on favourable terms so he could look after her. Right?'

Lisa nodded.

'In 2002 there'd been real controversy about an important vote in the Council Chamber. It was all over the Herdwick Gazette's front page at the time. Councillor Cedric Symons died in the meeting. Only your Dad saw what happened and he gave evidence to the Inquiry. His statement was crucial to the decision. He told me later in confidence that the Chairman of the Council was very grateful for his testimony. He didn't say anything to me about a promise of early retirement if he was patient but I bet that's what happened. I do remember him telling me on the quiet, well before I knew that he was to retire, that I should polish up for a possible interview for an important job vacancy that might be coming up. He'd smiled knowingly but wouldn't say anything else. It was some months later when he announced his departure.'

'You think that he did a deal in return for his evidence?'

'Yes, but Selwyn wouldn't have lied to the Inquiry so don't worry about that. He was dead straight. However he may have found a way to **not** say something, a way that suited his conscience. That's a negotiator's tactic. Nevertheless, he was a man of Deeds and Contracts. He liked things in writing, with certainty, with a guarantee. He wouldn't have been happy relying on a politician's promise with a vague timescale attached. He'd have wanted some backup to make sure it happened. The naked guy on his back on this desk looking over that woman's shoulder at the camera with a grin on his face was the Chairman of the Council at that time. I can't swear to the woman as we can only see her rear view but judging by the suspenders, stockings and stilettos I'd bet it was the Chief Exec's secretary. I can't remember her name but she was attractive in a sort of short-skirt, tight sweater, heavy make-up sort of way. I think Selwyn mentioned her in one of those e-mails. Would you believe it? Selwyn had the Chairman dead to rights - the dirty old dog!'

'But my Dad wouldn't resort to blackmail, surely?'

'Probably not, not normally ... but your Mam was ill. However, the Chairman wouldn't be in a position to risk it. He'd have Selwyn down as a hard-nosed, straight-talking property negotiator so he might have feared the worst. Anyway, Selwyn might never have shown him these photos. The Chairman may have delivered on his promise without any threats. As Selwyn still had the photos it's likely that he didn't need to use them otherwise he'd have handed them over to the Chairman once he was certain of his retirement. You only claim on an Insurance policy when something goes wrong. As I said, we'll never know. Still … you've got to admire Selwyn's plan … a deal-maker right up to his last day with the Council.'

'So what do I do with the photos now?'

Farah shrugged. 'Burn 'em. They've served their purpose. That Chairman died years ago. We're not certain who or where the lady is and I doubt she'd be happy to know they exist. Why risk anyone speculating on your Dad's reputation by saying how you got them? Anyway, as we said before about the e-mails, the Chairman's descendants won't thank you for seeing them, especially not in Selwyn's exhibition at the museum. Just don't set fire to them in here or you'll trigger the fire alarms. There's been enough hot action in this room over the years as it is.'

They both laughed.

***

Lisa went out through the Town Hall front door. She sat on the seat where Farah had told her that she'd talked with Selwyn on the night that he'd died. Her Dad's kingdom surrounded her. Streets bustling with tourists and locals, Shepdale Town Hall behind her, the Wandering Tup in front and Selwyn's beloved fells wrapped around everything, dotted with sheep. She tapped into her phone and instantly a Driverless Taxi unhitched itself from its charger higher up Sheepfold Lane, beeped its way backwards out of its bay and then angled its way down the street towards her. A gull-wing door lifted to allow her entry. Before she stepped inside she looked up at the electronic timeline across the front of the Town Hall:

15:05 Friday 24 October 2036: ... Breaking News ... Shepdale Museum honours well-known local character...

'He was certainly a character, even in a district full of them, but maybe it's just as well that they don't know all his secrets,' she thought. 'Sayonara, anjin-san.'

18: RIGHT PERSON, RIGHT PLACE, RIGHT TIME (1966)

Selwyn stepped off the main street and pushed his way through the double swing doors into the dark foyer of Shepdale Town Hall. The place was deserted even though it was mid-Monday morning. Very little sunlight penetrated its spacious interior. He let his eyes grow accustomed to the gloom. Ornate stone staircases, with cast-iron stair rails and smooth wooden bannisters on either side of the foyer, wound their way up to the floor above. An even darker corridor lined with portraits of former Councillors stretched away immediately in front of him. He could make out the embossed wording on the brass plaque of the nearest portrait - 'Walter Winster. Mayor, 1933-1938'. He studied the lacquered oak half-panelling along the entrance walls and the polished-oak parquet flooring and marvelled at the expense and craftsmanship that the Victorians had put into the place. A dark oak sign with gold lettering saying 'Council Chamber' was attached to the nearest face of the corridor wall pointing down that corridor into the inner recesses of the building. He'd visited the Town Hall before to attend Saturday night dances in the Assembly Room upstairs but he'd never been along that ground floor corridor and he wondered what it was like. As much as he wanted to, he didn't have the nerve to go wandering along it to find out.

Behind him were the rooms on either side of the main entrance that fronted onto Sheepfold Lane. A door to the nearest office, with 'Caretaker' etched into its glass panel, half-opened and a tall man with glasses and brylcreemed hair, wearing a khaki dust coat over his day clothes, leaned out and looked at him. Selwyn must have seemed a bit out-of-place.

'Can I help you lad?'

'I'm looking for the Borough Surveyor?'

The Caretaker nodded towards the door etched with 'Town Clerk' on it and smiled.

'You want Mr Arthur Croxteth. You'll find him in there. He said he was just popping in to leave a note for the Town Clerk.'

Selwyn coloured up a bit as if he should have known, said 'Thanks,' and went to knock on it.

'Come in.'

Selwyn turned the handle, pushed the door half open and leaned around it without entering. A man aged about mid-forties, wearing a tweed sports coat over a white shirt and tie was leaning over the desk with his back to the door.'

'Can I help you?'

'I'm looking for the Mr Croxteth, the Borough Surveyor.'

'You're lucky. You've found him. This isn't my office but come in and sit down anyway. If the Town Clerk comes back we may have to shift. What can I do for you?'

He sat down behind the desk. Selwyn took his first ever step inside a Council office and sat down opposite him.

***

It had been an exceptionally wet winter and spring in Herdwick district. Out on the fells the sheep huddled under the lee side of the stone walls to shelter from the driving wind and rain. It had been a poor lambing season. Rainfall high up in the Shepdale Horseshoe had sent torrents racing down its tributaries along the Shepdale Valley until they'd poured into the River Shep to cascade out into Herdwick Bay. Not all that water made it to the Bay. Along the way some of it overflowed onto the lower roads within Shepdale Town Centre. Three times the town centre had flooded, preventing traffic from passing through it on the main A road north, collapsing the road drains and undermining the tarmac road surfaces. There was a good reason that the old town buildings were built out of limestone and slate. The rains had come to remind everyone of that. Then suddenly in May it had stopped and the sun had come out. June looked set to be a glorious month – a much needed respite to allow the recovery to begin.

Selwyn hadn't been too bothered by the bad weather. He been busy studying for his A-levels at Shepdale Grammar School. When he wasn't studying he liked to get out on the fells and just walk. He'd spent plenty of his youth walking the footpaths and fells with his Dad. At sixteen, mainly for his own amusement and as a break from studying, he'd started going out on his own when his Dad was too busy with work. He'd begun to record routes that he followed, making notes about their features, producing pen and ink sketches of the interesting locations and even painting some in watercolours. He took snaps with his new Corona Coronet camera and developed and printed black and white photos in the attic of his parents' home which he'd turned into a makeshift darkroom. Now he had quite a collection of photos, notebooks and sketchpads.

One sunny Sunday morning at the beginning of June he set out to walk up the Shepdale Valley to see what damage the wet spring had caused. He caught a bus as far as he could and alighted when it reached the last settlement where it turned to make the journey back to Shepdale.

Then he set out to walk up the rough track leading from the last farm to the first summit in the Shepdale Horseshoe. He'd been this way several times before and knew that he would soon reach Reservoir Cottage. He'd read in the Herdwick Gazette that the cottage used to be occupied by people employed to maintain the adjacent reservoir and the upper reaches of the River Shep. Apparently that maintenance would continue but with external contractors employed by the Northshire Rivers Board instead. The cottage had become surplus to requirements and Shepdale Municipal Borough Council had recently bought it to use as an outlying base for hiking and climbing by the Council's Parks and Tourism Service in a joint health and well-being initiative with North Herdwick Rural District Council.

As he approached the deserted cottage he noticed that one of the chimney stacks, the one on its far end, had collapsed inwards, knocking a hole in the slate roof. It looked a sorry sight and was no longer weathertight. He pulled his camera from his rucksack and took some snaps.

***

'My name is Selwyn. I'm at Shepdale Grammar School. All lessons are finished now so I'm off revising until I go back in for my A-level exams. I thought that now might be a good time to come in and see you. I was out walking yesterday up the Shepdale Valley and I passed Reservoir Cottage. I'd read in the paper that the Council bought it recently.'

'Yes, that's right. Why does that interest you?'

'I just wanted to report some damage. The recent storms appear to have blown over one of the chimney stacks onto the roof. There's a hole in the slates and it's raining in. The top of the stack is in bits. I picked up a loose piece of the lime-mortar and it crumbled very easily so it looks to have weakened from old age. I just thought that you might want to know about it so that you can get it fixed before it causes more damage.'

'That's very helpful of you. Most people would have just walked past without reporting it.'

'Well I like old buildings, they're interesting. I don't like to see them in disrepair.'

'Which chimney stack was it, the near or the far one as you approach it from the farm end?'

'The far one. I can show you on a photograph. I developed these last night.'

Selwyn reached into his rucksack, pulled out his notebook filled with sketches and with some photos lodged within the pages. He sifted through the notebook and handed over two of them. Then he placed the open notebook on the edge of Arthur's desk so as not to lose his place amongst the pages. Arthur studied the photos and then asked,

'Can I keep these?'

'No problem. Are they helpful?'

Very. I can use them to organise making it safe and arrange a temporary cover for the hole with our contractors. This may save me a trip up there. I can also use them to lodge a provisional insurance claim. I can get the stack and roof sorted and then worry about any inside damage to ceilings and decorations later when I have more time. What with all the rain we've had I'm very busy sorting out other flood damage repairs as it is without taking the best part of a day to go up the valley to inspect this as well. The Council hasn't formulated any fixed plans for opening up the Cottage for use yet so it's not spoiling any intentions that they might have.'

'I'm glad to be of help.'

'That looks interesting. Mind if I have a look?' Arthur reached over, took the open note book and thumbed through the maps and notes and sketches. 'How long have you been doing this?'

'About three years, whenever I get the chance to wander up the fells.'

'This is really good work – very detailed ...very accurate ...very artistic. If I didn't know the area already I reckon that I could find my way up and down there very safely just by following your instructions. I've never seen anything quite like them before.'

'It's my own system. I do watercolours of the views as well but they're at home.'

'You should have these published. They'd make an excellent guide book. I have a friend at the Herdwick Gazette who might be interested if you'd like me to ask.'

'Well, I've never thought about it. Do you really think so? I've got a lot more stuff like this at home. Can I get back to you on that?'

'Certainly.' Arthur scribbled on a pad, tore off the page and handed it to Selwyn. 'Here's my name and phone number. You might make a bit of money. Help you out at Uni if you're thinking of going there in September.'

'I haven't decided about Uni yet. I've applied and had a couple of provisional offers to take a Geography degree subject to getting the grades at A-level but I'm not sure if that's what I want to do yet. I can't see Geography getting me a job at the end of it unless it's as a teacher, and I don't want to do that. I've got a temporary job loading and unloading wagons and baling fleeces in the Wool Depot at Herdwick Farmers' Cooperative. I'm going to think about what I want to do over the summer whilst I watch England host the World Cup.'

'Well think about my suggestion for the guide book. Give me a ring if you're interested. And thanks again for reporting the damage up at Reservoir Cottage.'

***

Selwyn's next visit to the Town Hall resulted in the Town Hall Caretaker redirecting him outside and down the yard at the side. There he found a small, three storey stone-built office block wedged between the rear of the Town Hall and the former terraced town-houses that stretched along the road running down the opposite side of the Town Hall from the yard. In the gap behind the offices was a cleared open, pot-holed gravel surface which served as the car park to the offices. He entered a small reception space. An attractive young woman directed him through a side door and led him to Arthur's office. Selwyn noted the desks and drawing boards and filing cabinets. People were busy chatting on telephones or studying papers. He liked the buzz of activity as he passed through.

'Thanks for coming. Please take a seat.'

Arthur indicated the chair opposite his desk.

Selwyn placed his rucksack on the floor by the chair and sat down.

'Coffee?'

'Please.'

The attractive receptionist was looking at Selwyn. 'Milk and sugar?'

He nodded and she left, closing the door behind her.

'How are you, Selwyn?'

'Just a bit nervous and excited after your phone call.'

'That's understandable but don't be. We might look a bit rough in here but we don't bite.'

Selwyn laughed and relaxed a bit.

'Right, Selwyn, first things first. You said on the phone that you're interested in publishing your maps and notes and sketches of your fell-walks as a series of guide books. I've fixed up for you to see my friend at the Herdwick Gazette. We can take a walk over there later if that's convenient. He'll tell you all about that once he's seen them.'

'That'll be fine. Thanks.'

'Before that I have a proposition for you, if you're interested. Have you thought any more about going to Uni?'

'Not really. The exams seem to be going fine. But, if anything I'd rather find a practical career, although I've not fixed on anything.'

'Well consider this. How do you fancy a career as a surveyor? I think that with your interest in geography, your obvious eye for detail, your skill at recording maps and routes and landscape and buildings that you have a natural aptitude for what we do here in the Borough Surveyor's Department. You know the local area. I already know that you're a responsible sort of lad from reporting the damage at Reservoir Cottage. And you seem to know a bit about building defects. Do you think that might be of interest?'

'Do you mean a job here, working for you?'

'Yes. I've been short-handed for a while and the storms have caused even more work and made things worse. I can't persuade the Town Clerk to take on the expense of anyone qualified but he has agreed to a trainee surveyor post to assist me with the estate management side of the Department. The money's not great to start with but it would be on an annual rising scale. You could exist on it if you continued to live with your parents.

The Council will pay your expenses to take a correspondence course in your own time with the Royal Institution of Chartered Surveyors supplemented with evening classes at Lanchester College of Technology, to get your qualification. You could also study in the office if we ever get any quiet times. I'd suggest taking the General Surveying option as the best fit for what I need you for. It would take you 3 years with exams combined with a minimum of two years on-the-job training. If you qualify straight off then, as long as you're over twenty-one by then, you could become a Chartered Surveyor.'

'What would I be doing?

'Anything relating to Shepdale MBC property. I'm a Building Surveyor but in the Surveying Department we tend to do a bit of everything. I'd be looking for you to specialise in estate management. Buying, selling, leasing, managing repairs and maintenance, accounting for running costs. As you progress you might be dealing with contractors, building alterations and improvements. Small jobs at first and gradually working your way in. Generally we sort out problems with property to keep the Council functioning. It's a mix of office work and outside work, travelling around the area to inspect land and buildings, meeting with people, preparing reports, valuing, negotiating and agreeing deals etc.'

'Would I be based here, in this office, with a desk and a chair?'

'Yes, and a telephone. Just outside that door.'

'When would you want me to start?'

Arthur looked at his calendar.

'I'll need a reference from your headmaster. I assume that's going to be straightforward. First you've got to finish your exams and wait for your A-levels results. You need to get a minimum of two passes to get on the RICS correspondence course by the way. Then, presumably, you'd have to work a week's notice on your summer job at HFC. How does the first Monday in September sound to you?'

'Don't you have to advertise the vacancy?'

'No. Charles Bowstead, the Town Clerk, trusts my judgement. I have authority to appoint anyone that I think fit. You're just the right person for us.'

'Well then, it seems like I'm the right person in the right place at the right time. Thanks.'

19: THE BANK CLOCK (1971)

Arthur, the Borough Surveyor of Shepdale Municipal Borough Council and his trainee, young Selwyn, were sitting in the window seat of the Wandering Tup pub on Sheepfold Lane in Shepdale town centre contemplating their half-empty drinks. Lunch for each of them was a mutton pie with mint gravy and pickles and a pint of Rampant Ram. The place was filling up, mainly with Council workers from the Town Hall across the road. Outside the sun shone from a cloudless late August sky but with noise and dust a constant irritant. Traffic jammed the street, which was the main A road north on the west coast of the country. Wagons ferried materials from the quarries through the town to supply the construction of the motorway extension running north from the end of the Lanchester by-pass and around the east side of Shepdale. The wagons competed for space with farm vehicles heading to and from the auction mart and abattoir, with delivery vehicles to the local shops and businesses and with tourists seeking a way to and from their holiday destinations. The town was rammed full as tourists and locals jostled for space on the pavements at the busiest time of day in the busiest period of the year.

Arthur broke their silent contemplation.

'The Town Clerk sent for me today.'

'Oh aye, what did he want?'

'He's been contacted by Ulverpool Urban District Council. They need some help.'

'What kind?'

'The professional kind. They need an RICS qualified negotiator for a tricky job. They're not a big enough Council to employ their own specialist and the nature of the job means that they don't want to commission a local surveyor – too much vested interest to be completely impartial.'

'What's that got to do with us?'

'The Town Clerk wants us to help them out. He

can't spare me and, anyway, I'm a Building Surveyor. They want a specialist negotiator who can certify a deal. As you've recently qualified as a General Surveyor he thinks that we can spare you for a few hours for as long as it takes. Ulverpool will pay to cover your hours plus expenses.'

'What's the job about?'

'Some dispute with the Landlord about repairing responsibility on one of their structures.'

'Sounds interesting, when do I start?'

'As soon as you like. The first task is to agree the brief, document an exchange of letters to record the arrangement and ask them to confirm that you're covered by their Council's insurance policy. I suggest that you get over to Ulverpool UDC as soon as you can. I've got a contact and phone number in the office.'

They both reached for their pints in a synchronised movement.

***

Ulverpool was a small market town further west around Herdwick Bay than Shepdale. It had a smaller local authority and with a smaller Town Hall. Unlike Shepdale, Ulverpool's Town Hall was not in the centre of town and had no clock tower above it. Sometime in the Victorian period, as the Herdwick District Savings Bank had a turret above its town centre premises, the UDC had asked the Bank for consent to install a town clock in that turret. A 999 years lease was arranged at a peppercorn rent and the Council as tenant agreed to take on all the repairs to the turret part of the building that housed the new clock. All was peace and harmony for the next hundred years.

***

'Donald Ruxton is a very tricky man to deal with.'

Cecil Knowles, the Senior Clerk to Ulverpool UDC, had set out the plans of the Bank and Clock turret on his desk in Ulverpool Town Hall. He was a mousy, little man with half-moon glasses perched on the end of his nose. He looked like he preferred sitting in smoke-filled Council rooms to climbing the external ladder and cat walk to inspect the clock turret but he'd climbed it nevertheless.

'He's the Chairman of the Board of the Bank. He won't listen to reason. He won't deal with anyone that he thinks is beneath him. He's arrogant and boorish and stubborn. There are not enough adjectives to describe the man – pompous, aggressive, bombastic and self-important – take your pick or take all of them. There's only one opinion that matters and that's his. I just cannot get anywhere with him. I did think of suggesting a 50:50 split but in the end I didn't bother as he is not for moving from his entrenched position.'

Selwyn could not imagine Cecil getting heated and falling out with anyone but here he was clearly agitated just from recalling his experience. They had been to climb the clock tower together to inspect the structure and to try and work out how the people who had drafted the lease clauses had imagined the repairing responsibilities would work. It was a tricky area because the wording of the relevant clause made the Council responsible for:

"the said District Savings Bank clock tower so far as the same is above the roof of the District Savings Bank Building with the necessary supports thereunder and the clock therein.'

The clock turret sat on two massive oak beams that spanned two walls within the bank at roof height. It was impossible to tell if the beams were there specifically to hold up the turret or were part of the roof since they fitted in with the nature of the surrounding construction where other similar beams had been used to support the roof. Both beams suffered from wet rot that had obviously been establishing itself over many years and the weight of the clock turret had caused them to sag at one bearing end, the turret now leaning to one side and in danger of crashing down into the street.

'My immediate advice is to have the pavement under the turret cordoned off whilst this dispute is resolved or someone may be killed. I don't think the occupants of the Bank building are in any immediate danger but it may be in your best interests to advise them to vacate the top floor offices just in case. Make sure that you put it in writing.

Cecil looked alarmed but nodded in agreement.

'Also, you need to check your insurance policy just in case.'

'Some good points, Selwyn. I'll arrange everything immediately.'

'Do you have an Architect and have you sought quotes for the cost of repairs'

'We have an Architect. He has written a report and obtained quotes. I'll get you that information before you go. The Council's opinion is that the beams form part of the roof and fall to the Bank to repair. The Bank's view is the opposite; that the beams support the turret so fall to the Council to repair. Legal opinion differs on both sides. We have reached a stalemate with discussions.'

'Let me have copies of everything that you think is relevant. After I leave here I'll call on Ruxton's secretary at the Bank and arrange an appointment to meet him.'

***

'A difficult customer, eh?'

Selwyn was sitting facing Arthur in Arthur's office. The door was closed.

'I'll say. He's everything we expected and more besides. He went red in the face and virtually threw me out of his office. I thought that he was going to have a heart attack. He really does have a very bad-temper. No wonder Cecil Knowles couldn't deal with him.'

'Not you, though. Everything went to plan?'

'I think so. He really didn't like dealing with someone as lowly as me. And especially as I gave as good as I got but, unlike him, without losing my temper. He now thinks that the UDC is as implacably entrenched as he is. That neither side will back down from expecting the other side to pay 100% of the repairs and professional fees and that we are heading for a very expensive Court hearing with barristers and the lot. I think that we've pushed him far enough. I can't see him getting much support from his Board when they hear what a legal action might cost.'

'So we're ready to move to phase two. I've briefed our Town Clerk. There's nothing like the threat of legal action to concentrate the mind. Can you draft the letter on his behalf and I'll give you a second opinion on it before we ask him to sign it? I have great faith in the power of the written word.'

'Will do.'

'Now, tell me, what's his secretary like? You must have made quite an impression to get that information out of her.'

'Jackie? Very nice. She's about my age, very attractive, quite bright and fortunately not in any relationship. We got chatting that first time when I called at the Bank to arrange a meeting with Ruxton. I took her to the Ulverpool Arms and bought her lunch and a couple of drinks. Can I put that on my monthly expenses claim as Ulverpool will be reimbursing us?'

'Why not. I'll sign it. It will be worth it to them if we get them a deal.'

'I'm seeing her again next Saturday so it wasn't as cold and clinical as you might think. It was more luck than anything. I didn't set out to tap her up for information. I think that I was pushing at an open door. She can't stand him as a boss. There's no love lost there. She's looking to transfer to the Shepdale branch if a suitable vacancy crops up. She'd rent a flat in Shepdale rather than travel if that happens, which might be good news for me. However, her saying that *'the rest of the Board would be happy to do a 50:50 split on the repairs in view of the ambiguous Lease wording and only Ruxton was proving to be the obstacle'* just came out in conversation. I sensed then that we needed to put some doubts in his mind with a very strong approach in our meeting. Then later we could show him a way out with honour intact, both with us and in front of his Board, by letting him appear to win. I'm hoping that he'll bite our hands off. It's like you've always taught me, half the skill of this job is about reading people. I know it's not guaranteed to work but he was never going to settle with me in a month of Sundays anyway. We can't make things worse by trying now that we know where the Board stands.'

'If we pull this off Selwyn I'll buy you a pint.'

***

SHEPDALE MUNICIPAL

DAVID LEWIS POGSON

BOROUGH COUNCIL

TOWN HALL, SHEEPFOLD LANE, SHEPDALE, NORTHSHIRE

TEL: Shepdale 44444

Please ask for Mr C Bowstead, Extn. 12

Mr Donald Ruxton Esq,

Chairman of the Board,

Herdwick District Savings Bank,

Market Street,

ULVERPOOL

Northshire   10th September 1971

My Dear Mr Ruxton,

In the matter of repairs to the Herdwick District Savings Bank Clock

I have had a report that you met with an Assistant Surveyor from this Council recently to discuss liability for the repairs to the Ulverpool Bank clock turret and that the meeting did not match up with your expectations. I have spoken to the individual concerned about how he conducted himself. He will no longer be involved with that case. You will not be expected to meet with him again. I offer my sincerest apologies without reservation on behalf of Shepdale MBC and Ulverpool Urban District Council if any offence was caused to you. It is not acceptable that a gentleman of your stature and standing should have had to deal with a junior member of my staff and had I known in advance of that intention then I would have ensured that the matter be handled by someone at a more appropriate level. I hope that you can accept that I have acted swiftly and responsibly in this aspect of our dealings.

Unfortunately any damage that has been done cannot be undone. However, the matter that brought about that unhappy meeting can still be resolved amicably. We are both gentlemen of equal stature and standing so it should be well within our joint gift to reach a mutually acceptable resolution to the matter of the clock turret repairs without the lengthy and expensive court proceedings that the Urban District Council now appears bent upon pursuing. Once that matter reaches Court any resolution will be out of our hands and the outcome will be uncertain at best. Being a Solicitor by qualification I have extensive experience of the legal system and can say with certainty that the whole Court process is no better than a lottery. I am sure that you, with all your experience, will concur with that view and acknowledge that it is better for both sides to avoid such an expensive risk and the damaging impact upon our reputations that will inevitably follow from such a public dispute between two prominent and respected institutions.

If, upon mature reflection, you Sir, are prepared to consider some movement on your part to resolve this matter then I think that I can prevail upon the Urban District Council to reconcile itself to accepting a reasonable indication of terms from you. I humbly venture to suggest that if you were to offer to meet half of the agreed cost of the repairs and associated professional fees then I would strongly urge the Urban District Council to accept such a magnanimous gesture on your part. That being so, I ask if you are willing to explore that possibility with your Board and persuade them of the advantages.

As things now stand, the condition of the clock turret continues to deteriorate, the danger to the public is increasing and the cost of repairs continues to rise. I believe that both sides are in agreement that action to repair the clock turret is urgently required. Whatever your reply, I am obliged to report it to the Urban District Council. The matter will then be considered by its full Council and that may well have to be in open session for democratic reasons. It is inevitable that any such discussions will be reported by the local newspaper despite any efforts on my part to suppress it. It is quite possible, no matter how unfair it may seem, that the Bank, including your good self, may be portrayed in an unfavourable light if it becomes apparent that the Council is willing to reach a compromise whilst you are perceived not to wish to do so. I would prefer to avoid placing you in such an unfair and invidious position. However, without any suggestion from you I cannot avoid that likely outcome as I am obliged to acquaint the Urban District Council with all that has been exchanged between us. Hopefully you can see your way towards helping me to prevent such unfortunate publicity in both our interests.

Your assistance in this matter, if you are minded to offer it, would be greatly welcomed and, as such, would be publicly reported to that Council in a very favourable light. You have my word upon it as a gentleman and I look forward to your reply.

I remain your obedient servant,

Charles Bowstead, LLB

Solicitor and Town Clerk for Shepdale Municipal Borough Council

***

Jackie smiled as she dropped her handbag onto the floor and wriggled onto the corner stool at the bar of the Ulverpool Arms. Selwyn took the other empty stool next to her.

'So ... a second date. I must be doing something right,' she said.

'Well, our lunch last time wasn't really a date, was it? That was more a spur of the moment thing or I might not have had the chance to see you again. I don't get out to Ulverpool much. What would you like to drink?'

'Well I'm glad that you asked me. Bacardi and coke please.'

The barman heard her and reached for the optic.

'How's work going?'

'A vacancy has come up at the Shepdale Branch. I've applied for it. I'll have to wait for a decision but I've already decided that I'll take it if I'm offered it.'

'And will you move to live in Shepdale?'

'Definitely. We'd be able to see a bit more of each other ... if you want to. By the way, did you hear if your Town Clerk got the reply from old Ruxton? I typed and mailed it about two days ago.'

Selwyn looked around to check who might be listening. No one in the pub seemed interested in their conversation but, nevertheless, he lowered his voice deliberately as he replied,

'Not yet. Are you allowed to tell me what it says?'

'He's offered the 50:50 split that Mr Bowstead suggested. I read Mr Bowstead's letter. Did you really get an awful telling off from the Town Clerk for upsetting Ruxton?'

Selwyn resisted the temptation to brag about his plan. He was learning that Jackie wasn't the most confidential person in the world.

'Water off a duck's back.'

20: THE KEY TO DEMOCRACY (1973)

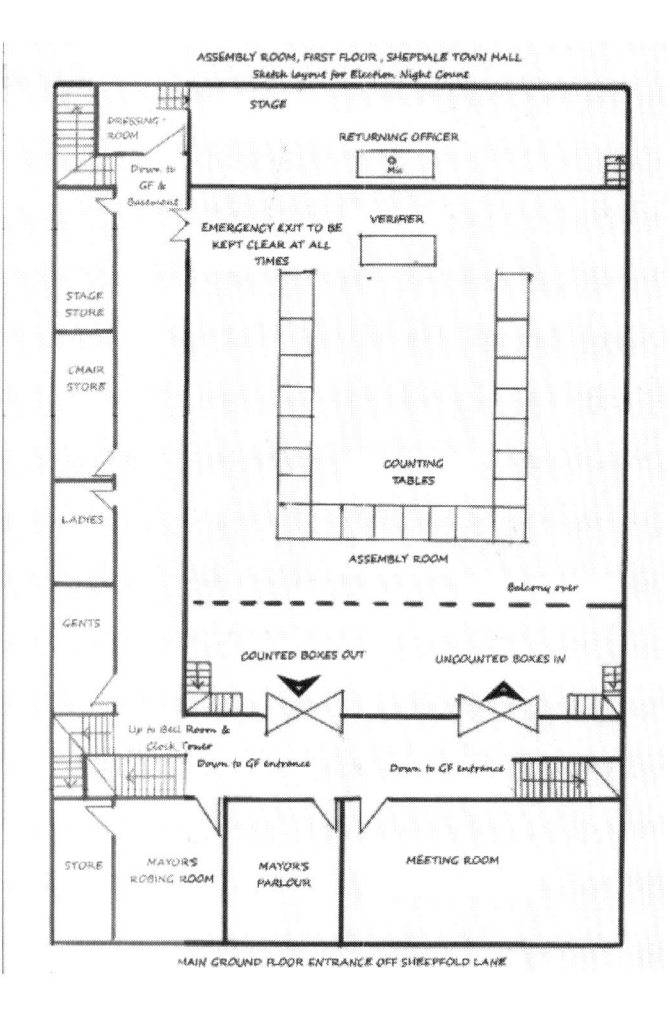

On a night of high emotion in the most important election ever held in Shepdale Town Hall, the least regarded member of the Election team was at the centre of a drama that almost caused the fledgling Herdwick District Council to not come into being. Not since the pre-war days of Walter Winster, when the renowned Herdwick dialect poet, brawling publican and occasionally-violent one-time Mayor of Shepdale had caused uproar in the Council Chamber, with his bid to prevent discussion to bring about restricted drinking hours in Shepdale, had the Town Hall seen such excitement. It was not a good start to the 1974 Local Government Reorganisation.

***

Selwyn had met Larry in 1966 in the first month of his career as a trainee surveyor in the Borough Surveyor's Department of Shepdale Municipal Borough Council. Arthur, Selwyn's manager, had handed Selwyn two files and said,

'You might as well jump straight in at the deep end, lad. This 'live' file is about a small parcel of surplus Council land that needs selling by tender. This 'dead' file shows how we sold a similar piece last year. Read the dead one and apply the same procedure to the live one. Come and ask me if you have any questions. Go and see Larry at the Bin Depot for some 'For Sale' signs, posts and a hammer. Just make sure that you tell him exactly what you want. Don't leave it up to him to think about details.'

Selwyn soon came to learn that every Council needed a Larry. The guy that everybody went to when a difficult, dirty and physical job needed doing. Larry wasn't the brightest spark at the Depot, didn't have any conversation apart from the odd grunt, laugh or 'Nar-then' in greeting but his capacity for hard graft was incomparable. He'd somehow learnt to drive in the 1950s when the roads were empty and the Driving Test might have been easier. He'd been with the Council since he'd left school and there wasn't a vehicle in the Depot that he couldn't drive. When the drains were blocked, the bins needed emptying or the potholes needed filling, no matter what the time or weather Larry would be out there doing it and he wouldn't quit until the job was finished. Selwyn had never met anyone who worked harder. But any instructions had to be made clear and simple with no room for interpretation of details. Larry was a literal person.

***

On the night of the Election Larry was drafted in to the Election Team and given just one job. Jim, the Admin Officer was working for Tom, the Senior Committee Clerk, who was working for

Charles Bowstead, the Town Clerk who was the Returning Officer in charge of the Election process.

Jim had taken the team, including Larry and Selwyn, to the first floor of the Town Hall and into the cavernous Assembly Room where Selwyn had attended dances as a teenager. It had a polished wooden floor, a stage at one end and an overhanging balcony at the other. It was now laid out for the Election Count. Jim wanted to familiarise them with the setup and take them through the count. Lots of folding tables arranged end-to-end in a U-shape filled the centre of the room. There were no gaps between the tables but the opening in the mouth of the U faced the stage at the far end of the room away from the main entrance doors. In that opening, under the stage and facing into the U, was the Verifier's table where Tom would sit. Another desk with a microphone was set up on the stage behind the Verifier for the Town Clerk to announce the results.

Jim showed Larry a typical black Ballot Box with a slot in its top for posting the voting slips. Boxes would be issued to each Polling Station to hold the votes. Then Jim took Larry through his job ready for the night.

'Larry, on Election night lots of Ballot Boxes like this from all over the district will be brought in here by the Poll Clerks from the Polling Stations via the main staircase. They'll be left just inside the entrance to this room. Somebody will be here to receive them. Now, you see those tables in the middle of the room? The boxes will be taken to those tables for the votes inside them to be counted. Ok, so far?'

A grunt and a smile from Larry. Jim continued,

'Then the voting slips will be put back inside, the lid will be shut and each counted box will be placed in another pile over here. Your job is to stack any counted boxes onto the caretakers' flatbed trolley, take them out and down the side corridor to the back stairs, carry them down in two's to the basement and lock them in the Solicitor's Deed Vault for security ready for bagging up tomorrow. Here's the key. Lock that Vault every time that you leave it. Otherwise the Boxes will just stack up here and get in the way. On the night the place will be packed with candidates, party officials, spectators, the Press and all sorts of hangers-on so we don't want any incidents. Is that straightforward enough?'

Another grunt and a smile.

'Thanks, Larry. That's it.'

Jim continued, talking now to the other Team Members,

'On the night I'll be floating around sorting out any practical problems as they arise. Most of you will be Table Bosses, each in charge of a section of those counting tables with a team of Counters - a mixture of typists, admin people and volunteers from the local branch of the Herdwick District Savings Bank who are skilled in counting and bundling banknotes. The Counters will sit at those tables on the chairs already placed inside the U, facing outwards. The spectators will watch the count take place from the opposite side of the tables around the edge of the room between the U and the Assembly Room side walls. Right, are you with me so far?'

The team members nodded and Jim continued,

'The Table Bosses will work inside the U. As the Ballot Boxes arrive you will collect them from over there and take them down the far side to that space inside the counting tables. Each ballot box will be identified by Ward Name with a printed address taped on the lid, like this example. Each Ward will have at least one full Ballot Box, or sometimes two and occasionally three together if they are really big Wards. The Table Boss takes the Box or Boxes for one Ward only at a time to his section of tables, cuts the seals and empties the voting slips onto the tables. Ok so far?

The Table Bosses nodded.

'Your Counters will just count the total number of slips and note that down at first. The Table Boss will scribble that on a bit of paper and take that total along with its Ward identity to Tom to verify that the slips in the box match the total number of slips recorded as issued for voting that day by the Poll Clerks in that Ward's Polling Station. Still with me?'

Nods again from the team.

'If that overall total is verified by Tom then the Counters can spread the votes out again on the table and count them into bundles of fifties for each separate candidate standing in that Ward.. Each bundle of fifty will need a rubber band around it with any odd votes fastened on top with a paper clip. The Counters will have to look for potential spoilt votes and the Table Boss will take them to Tom for a decision. Table Bosses also have to watch for errors in the bundles. When you're happy with the bundles for each candidate you will note down the separate totals and then take them to Tom for recording.'

Jim checked again that they understood.

'If the totals for the all the candidates in that Ward all add up to the verified overall total then Tom will accept the count for that box. There might be recounts for close results. However, most should be clear cut. When the candidates accept the result then you can put the relevant bundles of votes back into the box and deliver it to Larry's collection point for removal to the Vault. The Town Clerk will then announce the result for that Ward. It might seem complicated but it should be fool-proof. Pens, notepads, scissors, paperclips and rubber bands will be put out on the tables ready for you. The public are not allowed to touch the boxes or the votes under any circumstances. Any questions?'

***

Selwyn had assisted at other local elections for Shepdale MBC since starting his career at the Council but his role as Table Boss was his first promotion from Counter and he had never been involved in anything as large as this. Jim, although younger than Selwyn, had far more Election experience and responsibility as it constituted an important part of his job description.

Similar elections were taking place all over the country in a complete shake-up of local government boundaries and responsibilities. Along with all the other new County Councils the new Northshire County Council had already been elected on the 12th of April 1973.

The new Metropolitan Districts had followed on 10th of May. Now it was the turn of the new District Councils. All across the country the old, small Municipal Borough, Urban and Rural District Councils – like Shepdale MBC, Lantern-o'er-the-Bay UDC, Ulverpool UDC, Winander UDC, North Herdwick RDC and South Herdwick RDC - would disappear on 31st of March 1974.

The new Herdwick District Council would be elected on the 7th of June 1973, and, in accordance with the Local Government Act 1972, would then shadow the old Councils until replacing them as those old Councils disappeared forever on 1st of April 1974

Selwyn was excited by the changes but also concerned about his job. He wasn't married but had lived with Jackie in her flat since she'd transferred to the Herdwick District Savings Bank branch in Shepdale from Ulverpool. Now she was dropping hints about getting married. He wasn't sure about marriage to Jackie.

At the back of his mind he'd always been a little concerned about her lack of loyalty her old boss Donald Ruxton when she'd worked at the Ulverpool branch. He knew that the outspoken comments she'd revealed to Selwyn at their first meeting were not an isolated incident. She had a tendency to blurt things out in conversation, including stuff that he told her about his work with the Council that he preferred not to be aired in public. Shepdale was a small town and keeping confidences was difficult enough at the best of times. Selwyn liked to maintain an outwardly professional public facade no matter what he might really be thinking on the inside. Jackie was less circumspect. Continually having to be careful what he said around her in case she passed it on was becoming a bit of a strain.

Anyway, he had no guarantees of employment under the new authority. There was a lot of talk inside the Council about early retirements for the older employees and promotion opportunities to newly created posts for the younger ones. His preference was to continue working for and with Arthur as part of any new Herdwick District Council Surveying Department but even Arthur couldn't guarantee what was in store for either of them. So marriage was a risk in those circumstances and Selwyn welcomed the opportunity to stall Jackie with that excuse.

***

Election Night on the 7th of June 1973 was frenetic. There were 54 seats to count. It had started slowly enough. Selwyn arrived at 9:30 pm with the polls due to close at 10pm. Jim had warned him that it might take until midnight or 1:00 am to finish. He'd told Jackie not to wait up and that he'd tell her all about it when he got home. She knew the girls from the Bank who were helping with the count so she was quite interested in what they were doing.

Around 10:15 pm the first boxes from the nearest Polling Stations started to arrive and the count began. The power struggle for control of the new Council had generated far more interest than the usual local elections. The Assembly Room was crammed with people which made it difficult for the Polling Clerks to get the boxes into the room and difficult for the Table Bosses to collect them from the entrance and carry them into the middle of the U.

By 11:00 pm the boxes were arriving faster than they could be cleared so began to stack up around the entrance. Charles Bowstead, the current Town Clerk, was announcing the results for each Ward as they were counted, the crowd was getting excited and the race for control of the new Council was well and truly under way.

No-one knew exactly what had happened. It had built up to a tense finish by twelve-thirty when the boxes from the outlying Wards finally arrived. They were dealt with at rapid speed despite numbed minds and tired feet. The running result showed a likely 'hung' Council with a neck and neck race between the Tories and the Liberals to be the largest party without an overall majority. They had an equal number of seats and it was all down to the last box to be counted from the Ulverpool Farside Ward. That box must have been delivered as its paperwork was with Tom. All the counted boxes had been cleared and stored in the vault. Someone, nobody knew who, had already said to Larry,

'That should do it, Larry. Thanks. I guess after that last load you can call it a night unless you want to stay for the announcement of the final result.'

Larry wasn't interested in who had control of the Council. It made no difference to him who was in charge. There would always be drains to clear or potholes to fill regardless. He'd decided to go, walked up from the basement to the ground floor and out onto Sheepfold Lane. Upstairs in the Assembly Hall they were just then discovering that the Farside box was missing.

There was a lot of huddled discussion between the Town Clerk, Tom and Jim. The Poll Clerk for the missing box was contacted by phone from the Town Clerk's office downstairs. He was roused from his bed and made to check the boot of his car. He confirmed that he'd delivered the box. His paperwork was on Tom's desk along with his record of voting slips issued and placed together with the few postal votes that Tom already held for that Ward. People could remember the Poll Clerk coming in with the box. But where was it? It could be a matter for the Police. This was an attack on democracy. The result could not be called.

After a search of the building, the only sensible conclusion was finally arrived at. That the box had got into the wrong pile in the heat of the finish. That Larry had taken it to the Vault by mistake. No-one could blame him for just doing his job but Larry, oblivious to the panic, had gone home with the Solicitors' key because no-one had thought to ask him for it back. He was a literal person. And nobody in the room was friendly enough with him to have either his address or phone number.

Until Selwyn quietly stepped forward and whispered to Jim,

'I've got a key. The spare key. The Legal Section got so fed up with me moaning at them to provide information from the Property Deeds stored in the Vault that they loaned me the spare on a permanent basis so I can go in there to do my own research. If the Town Hall Caretaker can let me into my office in the Surveyor's Department now I can fetch it from my desk.'

'Ok, but do it quietly. We don't want this getting out. I'll tell the Town Clerk.'

***

Things came to a head between Jackie and Selwyn after the Herdwick Gazette published the 'inside' story from an undisclosed source the following week. It may have been someone else who'd leaked it but Selwyn had gone home tired after the Count and made the 'mistake' of telling her about the key when she'd asked if anything exciting had happened. He'd made her promise to keep it under her hat. Later, when he asked her, she hadn't denied bragging to the girls at the Bank about how her Selwyn had saved the day. It was one too many times for Selwyn. He felt a little guilty but it was her own fault and it did give him his way out. They weren't engaged or anything. It was the 1970s. The days of suing for breach of promise were over anyway. He'd convinced himself it was for the best.

'Did I tell her deliberately to force the issue?' he asked himself later as he wrestled with his conscience. *'I could justify it as a negotiator's tactic ... to plant the story and see where it led. She'd chosen to reveal it after all.'*

Either way, he'd moved back in with his parents again by the following week.

21: THE RACE FOR INDE-PENDENCE (1976)

(Photo by kind permission of Frank Walker)

'Just because I married a farmer's daughter, work for her wealthy land-owning father and live in a cottage on his farm doesn't mean that I've forgotten my townie roots. I've still got a trick or two up my sleeve. I could outsmart them when I was at Shepdale Grammar School and I can still do it now. So will you join in with me?'

Selwyn and Ron, his elder brother, were sitting in the lounge of their parents' home where Selwyn had moved back to about three years ago when he'd split up with Jackie. Ron's obviously pregnant wife Mary was sitting outside talking to Selwyn's parents in the garden at the rear of their house in Shepdale.

'Ok, big brother. If you insist, but don't you think that you're getting a little too old for this kind of thing now that you're in your thirties and about to become a dad.'

'Not at all. It'll be good fun and I've got a plan. If it comes off then I'll be able to crow about it to those farm lads for the next two hundred years. It doesn't seem to matter that I've been involved with farming for the last fifteen years, they still see me as a townie off-comer. This will show them what town boys can do.'

'Don't you think it's too hot for physical effort?'

'No. You'll enjoy it.'

'That's not like you farmers. The weather is never right for you. Usually it's too hot or too cold, too wet or too dry, too windy or too calm.'

'This isn't farming. Anyway, we can cool off with some Rampant Ram in the pub afterwards. There'll be a bit of a do with food later. It'll make a change for you from the Wandering Tup. There'll be girls there too. Mary might get you fixed up.'

'Oh God, no!'

'Well you're 28 and still living with your parents. It's time that you met someone and moved out.'

'I've tried that. It didn't work out. And hark at you. At least I'm not trying to impress a bunch of farm lads. I think I'll give it a miss.'

'Too late, you've already agreed.'

***

As the crowds gathered to surround the competitors on the 'Horn of Plenty Inn' car park Selwyn could see the village green behind them. Its grass was burnt brown by the sun. Dust scuffed up as people walked across it to join them. There were a few American accents amongst the spectators. Selwyn and Ron were wearing giant white nappies, made out of bath towels, pinned over their shorts. It was a requirement of the entry rules. Villagers pointed and laughed and shouted wisecracks but they smiled and stayed silent, maintaining their concentration, studying their opponents; waiting to come under starter's orders. The competition looked beatable. The village boys and the farm lads were handicapped with heavy prams or push chairs with small wheels.

'No-one has a racing pram like ours,' whispered Ron.

'Right – let's be having you. All entries for the men's pram race line up along here.' The starter was pointing to a line chalked across the car park's tarmac surface.

Ten pairs of men shuffled forward. Selwyn was pushing the pram, his brother was riding and Selwyn deliberately chose the nearest starting point to the first obstacle about twenty five yards away. It was the kissing gate that led onto the narrow public footpath through the housing estate before opening into the Long Field.

The noise of expectation rose. Passing cars pulled into the side of Main Street and passengers alighted to watch. The crowd grew as stragglers rushed down the village to join them and drinkers wandered out through the pub doorway to swell the rear ranks. Selwyn leaned on the coach springs and tensed.

'Ready …get set …GO!'

He'd taken the strain, anticipating the signal, and pushed away to a flyer, making it first to the kissing gate and completely blocking it whilst he and Ron lifted their pram over the top. The other teams queued up behind them. They'd got their strategy right so far and were looking good for victory if they could maintain the lead. They knew it wouldn't be easy against the very fit farm lads.

***

Local Government Reorganisation had been a challenge over the last two years but Selwyn felt that the new organisation was bedding in at last. Arthur was the Head of Property Services with Selwyn as Estates Surveyor under him. Selwyn now had his own assistant and far more property to manage over a greater geographical spread arising from the merger of the old Councils into the new and larger Herdwick District Council. His other friends had survived too. Jim had become the new Assistant Committee Clerk to Tom, who remained Senior Committee Clerk despite the hiccup at the 1973 Election, and Eric had been retained in Finance.

The spring and summer of 1976 seemed set to be the warmest since records began. Lawns shrivelled and died, the leaves on the trees turned brown and fell early. Hosepipe bans were introduced and the Government issued advice about saving water ... 'share a bath with a friend' being one of them. Selwyn wasn't really convinced that he wanted to share one with Arthur, Jim or Eric.

It was unbearably hot in the old Shepdale Council Offices at the rear of the Town Hall, with no air-conditioning. The staff took it in turns to buy ice creams for each other every day. The dress code was relaxed to permit removal of ties except when attending Council meetings. A pint of Rampant Ram in the Wandering Tup with Arthur at lunchtimes was essential to Selwyn's survival. Jim, who felt he owed Selwyn something for saving the Election Team from complete embarrassment at the 1973 Election, and Eric from Finance, who just liked beer, now joined them on a regular basis. Despite the intense heat Selwyn had never been happier in his work and whistled to himself as he strolled down the Town Hall yard to the offices each morning.

Unusually, Selwyn avoided the fells in his free time because it was just too hot for comfortable walking. It didn't stop the tourists who continued to test the limits of the Herdwick Mountain Rescue Team, with dehydration being the cause of most call-outs. Even the hardy Herdwick sheep out on the fells struggled in the drought as the streams dried up and the farmers brought them down to the lowlands. They sheared them early and tankered in water to help them survive. Selwyn still had his doubts about strenuous physical effort in those extreme conditions but Ron wouldn't hear about him backing out.

That summer coincided with the 200 years anniversary of the American Declaration of Independence which had happened on the 4th of July 1776. It seemed a little strange to Selwyn that two neighbouring English villages within

Herdwick district should want to celebrate the loss of Britain's biggest colony from the Empire. But nobody held grudges, especially since the Americans had helped Britain out in two World Wars in more recent times. And the American tourists brought in income when they came to visit the church.

Ron and Mary farmed near one of the villages and intended joining in with the joint celebrations. The Parish had a historic connection with the estate owned by George Washington's ancestors. The Washington family's coat of arms was carved into the church wall. It was that coat of arms which had formed the basis for the 'Stars and Stripes' flag which now flew over the Church located halfway along the road under the crag between the villages. All week that flag had hardly fluttered above its tower with only the occasional breath of air to stir it.

A programme of events had been planned with the highlight being the pram race across the fields on the 2nd of July, the nearest Saturday afternoon to the Independence date. The pram-race course was from the 'Horn of Plenty Inn' located in one village to 'The Shepherd's Crook' pub in the other. It was about one and a half miles between them, following the public footpath leading directly across the level fields.

From the 'Horn's' car park the competitors could

see the other village in the distance, nestling on top of a small hill. The 'Shepherd's' car park was on the far side of that hill and spectators would be able to watch the start at the 'Horn' and then drive around the edge of the fields on the road past the Church beneath the crag to watch the finish on the other car park.

In the weeks leading up to the race Ron had found an old coach-built pram in his barn. The chrome was rusty and its fabric coverings were worn and faded. There was no way that Mary would allow him put their expected baby in it so it was surplus to requirements. He'd stripped it down to its chassis. The hood and tub had been disposed of, to be replaced with a plank bolted straight on to the fixed axles to form a base for sitting on. He'd cut off the pram handle with a hacksaw. The curls of the redundant coach-springs at each end were retained. In all, it was now a lightweight, low-slung racing machine with no unnecessary features.

One evening in the week before the race Ron had made Selwyn walk the route with him to assess the problems that might arise from the footpath surfaces and how they could over-come the variety of gates separating the fields that provided obstacles along the route. Then Ron got his brother to join him on his driveway for a short, slow-motion trial to rehearse their change-overs.

'Don't you think that you're taking this a bit too seriously?' was Selwyn's question.

'We have to win. It's a matter of pride.'

'Won't it be a bit uncomfortable without suspension?'

'We'll be fine. It'll only average out at ¾ of a mile each sitting down. You can stand it for that long.'

'What about steering?'

'The passenger sits looking forward on the plank holding onto the front curl springs to stay on. The pusher holds the rear curls and steers as he pushes. I've removed the brake as we won't be parking a baby in it ever again. Are you happy now?'

'It'll never work.'

'Of course it will. Light and fast for lifting over gates and pushing. You'll see.'

***

The run along the length of the Long Field and the small field beyond it towards the next village saw them increase their lead. The other prams just couldn't match their speed. They changed over from pusher to passenger regularly as they tired but, looking back, they could see the others struggling with their unaltered carriages as they fell further behind. Selwyn started to relax because the race was in the bag but Ron urged him on, keen to impose as crushing a defeat as possible on the others. The final gate to bring them alongside the old quarry and onto a decent gravel surface was no problem and Ron's 6' 3" rugby-player's physique soon had them speeding along the edge of the village playing fields. Only the final leg up through the village streets and down to the pub car park remained before a welcome pint to celebrate victory on a blistering hot day.

Ron called out, 'Racing change' as he tired.

He slowed, Selwyn jumped off and Ron kept pushing. Selwyn spun behind him and took over his pushing position as Ron dashed ahead, ready to climb aboard. That's when the heat-induced madness set in. As Selwyn slowed to let him on board Ron inexplicably launched himself into the air in a flying sideways leap, landing his full weight squarely on the plank seat. The bearings collapsed, the wheel rims buckled and the spokes pinged out sideways like scarifiers. The axles bowed and the whole chassis ground to a shuddering halt as the bottom of the pram thudded onto the floor in a cloud of dust and gravel. Ron rolled off the plank, picked himself up and helped Selwyn to straighten up from where his skinned and bleeding knees still rested on the gravel floor.

'Sorry, little brother.'

Their race was over.

They looked at each other. Selwyn laughed at the hopelessness of the situation. Ron sighed. Discussion was unnecessary. Together they lifted the remains of the pram to carry them up and over the last hill to the pub as the other competitors closed the gap. However, such was their lead that, even when just walking, they still finished before any of the others. But they knew that they were disqualified for being unfit to race. It didn't matter, it would be a better tale to laugh about later over a pint than if they'd won.

'The farm lads will have a field day now,' said Ron.

The crowd laughed and cheered as they walked in. A very pregnant Mary was holding out a pint of Rampant Ram for Ron. Standing next to her was the most stunning girl that Selwyn had ever seen. And the vision was holding out a sorely-needed pint towards him.

'Hello Mary, still looking swell as usual,' said Selwyn, his eyes still on the vision. 'No nearer producing that baby yet?'

'I was hoping the excitement of watching you two race today might move things along but after hearing about that pathetic finish, no chance!'

'Thanks for the pint err ... what's your friend's name?'

'This is Megan, Selwyn. She knows who you are. She was at school with you although a few years below. She remembers having to watch you play rugby for the School 1st XV on Wednesday afternoons. Don't you recognize her?'

'You'd think that I should have remembered that.'

'Nice outfit, not as attractive as your rugby strip though,' Megan laughed, pointing at the giant nappy. 'It reminds me of work.'

'What work?'

'I'm a nurse at Northshire Herdwick Hospital. I've just moved back to the village after working down south.'

'We met when I went to maternity for a check-up. I invited her to join us today,' said Mary, looking very intently at Selwyn for a response.

'I'm pleased that you did.'

***

The evening in the Pub was a great success. Hunger was satisfied and thirsts were quenched.

The farm lads thought that Ron and Selwyn's disastrous race was hilarious and asked them to tell and re-tell the story continuously in the crowded bar. Selwyn noticed that he and Ron hardly had to buy any drinks. With each re-telling the farm lads thrust another pint each into their hands and Ron embellished the tale until it was cemented into local legend. By the end of the night, he had Selwyn and himself 'three fields ahead of the pack' and his sideways leap included enough twists and somersaults to win the diving gold medal at the Olympic pool.

In a rare quiet moment Selwyn whispered to Ron,

'Surprisingly, I think our failure in the race has earned you the outcome that you wanted. The farm lads seem to have accepted you, Ron'

'I told you that I had a plan, Sel.'

'It seems that you were right, even if it worked out for all the wrong reasons.'

'What wrong reasons? It worked. Anyway, I told them that it was really all your crazy townie idea and that I never thought it would work.'

Megan asked, 'What are you two laughing about?'

Selwyn, with enough beer inside him now, seized his opportunity,

'Just remarking on what a good day it's been. By the way, what are the chances of me seeing you again after tonight?'

'Well, if you're thinking of continuing with pram racing then there's every chance that I'll see you in the hospital with more damage than skinned knees. Otherwise you'll just have to ask me out.'

'Tell me Megan. If I did end up in hospital would you tell everyone about my injuries?'

'I wouldn't be allowed to – patient confidentiality.'

'That's good to know,' thought Selwyn. *'I like a woman who can keep my confidences.'*

22: THE GREAT SHEPDALE BELL (1979)

'Do you remember Mad Mike who used to work in the Environmental Protection Group at Herdwick District Council?'

Selwyn had called in to Shepdale Museum at the

end of Sheepfold Lane on his way from visiting Megan and his baby daughter Lisa in the maternity unit at Northshire Herdwick Hospital. He was sitting opposite Sheila in the Curator's office.

'Vaguely. Environmental Protection Group never visited us much. Was Mike the guy who was involved in the Shepdale Bell dispute last year? The one whose hair turned white overnight. I seem to remember his name from reports of the controversy in the Herdwick Gazette.'

'That's him. He went off sick after that and never came back to work. I ran in to him last night when I went to wet the baby's head with Arthur, Jim and Eric at the Wandering Tup.'

'Oh, yes. How is Megan ... and the new baby? Congratulations. A girl I believe. The grapevine never sleeps in the Council.'

'Both doing well. 7 pounds 12 ounces. We're calling her Lisa. She looks just like her mother, fortunately.'

'That's lucky. Give Megan my love.'

'Anyway, as I was saying. Mike came wandering in. We all chatted. He works for Lanchester City Council now but still lives in Herdwick district. He's been receiving counselling since his sudden departure from the Council. As part of his treatment he told us that he'd been advised to try and confront his fears. He told me how he was approaching that. Apparently visiting the Wandering Tup last night was a big step forward in his recovery but that was as near as he wanted to get to the Town Hall across the road. He kept glancing at it through the front bay. I don't think that he'll ever set foot in there again. Strangely, he had a pocketful of bits of paper, all with the same words on them, written out by him. He was giving them out to everyone in the pub. Said it was his mission now. That was also part of his therapy, he said, and he gave me this copy.'

Selwyn handed her a piece of paper with words scribbled on it and said,

'It sounds familiar to me, like a bit of the famous Walter Winster's dialect poetry, but not familiar at the same time if you know what I mean. Arthur said the same thing. We were curious. We thought that you Sheila, as the local Winster expert, might know what it was.'

Sheila read it quickly and smiled.

'I know what the words could be. I wouldn't have known it six months ago. I'm amazed that Mike has a copy though. Including the workmen and the Landlord of the Tup, there's only a handful of people in the world who've seen this before. Hang on a minute.'

She walked over to a filing cabinet, unlocked it, opened the top drawer and pulled out a clear plastic envelope containing what looked like an unfolded Capstan Full Strength Navy Cut cigarette packet. Turning the envelope over she handed it to Selwyn and said,

'Handle this carefully. Please don't take it out of the plastic. Just read that side. Then tell me exactly what Mike said to you.'

***

The Great Shepdale Bell had hung in the old Moot Hall at the crossroads on Sheepfold Lane since the fifteenth century. Locals claimed that it had been rung by hand every hour on the hour both day and night since then. It was reputed to bring good luck to the district just so long as it continued to ring out. It could be heard out on the fells. The Herdwick shepherds used it to find their way down after dark or in times of poor visibility from fog, rain and snow ... which was often. In the main, the good luck had held as the town had prospered from the wool trade and from peaceful times as the great domestic upheavals of British history - the War of the Roses, the Civil War, the Jacobite Rebellion - all passed Herdwick district by.

In Victorian times the Moot Hall had burnt

down. A town subscription raised funds to replace it with a new Town Hall on the same site. A clock tower was added on top and the Great Shepdale Bell was re-hung behind the clock in the Bell Room with the striker rope hanging directly down through the ceiling into the Council Chamber below ready for hand-ringing. Immediately behind the dangling rope, on the Council Chamber wall, a carved wooden plaque spelt out the now-redundant Shepdale Municipal Borough Council motto *"Pannus mihi Passionis"* and beneath it the last verse of Walter Winster's world famous dialect poem, **'Ode to t'Erdwick'** ...

"Tis t'grandest sight a man can see

Yon 'erdwicks oot on't fell.

Then us knows thars scran on't table

An' all with England's well."

In later years the Bell's striking mechanism was converted to electrical power and the hand-pulling on the rope was abandoned. From above the Town Hall the Great Bell continued to sound out across Shepdale and out onto the fells as Herdwick district emerged unscathed from two world wars and looked forward to renewed prosperity from the international expansion of nostalgia-inspired tourism in the second half of the twentieth century.

In 1978 the Bell faced its greatest threat since the Moot Hall fire.

***

Selwyn continued to recount his evening with Mad Mike to Sheila.

'You remember that long running dispute about the Shepdale Bell last year? That's what sent Mike mad. Some off-comer bought the 'The Olde Smoke-Shed Guest House' in the town centre and immediately made a fuss about his guests and himself not being able to sleep with the noise from the bell striking the hours through the night. Mike had to go up to the Bell Room above the Town Hall and take sound measurements with a decibel counting machine. It was well in excess of 85dBA so he had to advise the Public Health Committee that the loudness of the Bell constituted a statutory nuisance under the Public Health Act 1936 and had to be abated at night. And what a row followed that. Committee meeting after Committee meeting, Councillors up in arms, petitions, marches, a protest with sheep herded through the town, farmers chaining themselves to the historic hitching rings outside the Town Hall, letters to the Herdwick Gazette, letters to the local MP, a question raised in Parliament. All claiming an attack on our rights, sweeping away centuries of tradition, disrespecting our history, off-comers not understanding northern ways, disaster likely to befall the district and so it went on. Mike was under a lot of stress as everyone blamed him just as much as the off-comer.'

'I remember it well. We did a small feature exhibition about it in the Museum for the schoolkids at the time.'

'Charles Bowstead, the Clerk and Chief Exec, sent for Arthur and asked Property Services to find a solution. And we did. We talked to Shepdale Bellmakers & Clockmenders Ltd. They suggested that we record the sound of the Bell and appoint them to fit an electronic sound system in the Bell Room. They fitted a timer mechanism to shut off the automatic Bell striker at night whilst the recording kicked in to play it through speakers at a lower decibel level. It was a compromise that complied with the law but pleased nobody. Locals round here are never happy unless they have summat to moan about. One unfortunate consequence was that the Bell could no longer be heard out on the fells above the noise from the new Motorway. But it was the best that we could do in the circumstances. Charles told the Councillors that they would just have to lump it or end up losing in Court. The row died down eventually but it may yet pop up again come the next local election.'

'I guess that the Council was caught between

two crooks. So what exactly happened to Mike?'

'Well, after we fitted the new system, he had to go back to the Bell Room at midnight one Friday night to verify the lower decibel level. Nobody knows how it happened but the door jammed shut behind him and he was locked in there alone until Monday morning when the Caretaker found him. By that time his hair had turned white and he was rambling. That was the last that we saw of him until last night.'

'So how did he come up with the writing on this slip of paper?'

'Well Mike reckons that whilst he was locked in the Bell Room he was visited by the ghost of Walter Winster. We're not sure about that really because who believes in ghosts? And, anyway, there was a portrait of Walter Winster stored in that room. It could have played tricks with his mind. You know all those pictures of past Mayors that line the corridor leading to the Council Chamber in Shepdale Town Hall? Well we'd run out of space for any more so we'd taken the first one down to hang the picture of the current Chairman of Council in its place. Our intention is to work our way along the wall in date order in the future as new Chairmen are appointed. The portrait that we'd taken down just happened to be Walter's from when he was Mayor. I recall it well because it was the first thing that I saw when I visited the Town Hall in 1966 at the start of my career. We stored it in the Bell Room. Mike had nothing else to look at or to talk to for the whole of that weekend.'

'It must have been horrible.'

'Well yes … Walter wasn't a great-looking bloke judging by that portrait. Oh, sorry … you mean about Mike being locked in? Yes, that must have been horrible too. You know about Walter's history - falling off the Tup roof just across the road and dying as a result on VE day in 1945. There's some old Tup-regulars that claim to have seen his ghost crossing Sheepfold Lane to the Town Hall at throwing-out time. They reckon that Walter goes over there to climb the Clock Tower for a better chance of winning his bet that he can see Blackpool Tower off the higher roof. Can ghosts see at night? Maybe it's only when Blackpool Illuminations are on. Really, I just put that down to the regulars having had too much Rampant Ram of a Saturday night.'

'Don't you believe in ghosts Selwyn?'

'I don't, but Mike does now. He reckons that Walter spoke to him over and over again that night in the Bell Room, with the recorded Bell ringing in his ears every hour at night, repeating what's written on that bit of paper…

'But hark t't warning yan an' all

'Bout 'erdwicks oot on't fell.

Yons' luck will only last s'long

As't earing t'Shepdale Bell.

So, Sheila, where did the cigarette packet come from with those same words written on it?'

'That's the funny thing about all this. It was only found earlier this year under the floorboards of the Wandering Tup. Workmen were re-insulating the void with fleeces in keeping with its original construction, to comply with its Grade II* listing. They were fixing a bit of wet rot that was discovered in the floor joists. It was well-after the date when Mike was locked in the Bell Room. You'll be aware that Walter was landlord at the Tup up to the date of his death. We've had the phrasing and handwriting examined and it seems to be Walter's. We also have a box of his original notes donated to the Museum by his widow. The academics like to study them to see how Walter developed his inspiration although I think that he was just three sheets to the wind when he was writing. He drafted most of his stuff on the back of Capstan Full Strength Navy Cut fag packets – his smoke of choice apparently – whilst sitting in the Tup. We reckon that he wrote this as the intended final verse to his world famous **'Ode to t'Erdwick'**. Then, because he was drunk, dropped this very cigarette packet on the floor when he stood up … or fell over … or passed out. It must have slipped between a crack in the floorboards and we guess that he'd forgotten that he'd written it when he'd sobered up. It's ironic …the original Herdwick fleeces must have preserved it from the damp.'

'So Mike can't have seen it.'

'Not really. It's not been made public yet. We won't release it until we're certain of its provenance. It will have world-wide interest for Walter's fans. Especially with that emerging Greenpeace organisation where he has a bit of a cult following.'

'That poetic reference to 'luck' not lasting if you can't hear the Bell on the fells – I know it's been a local superstition as long as I've been around - that does seem to fit with the other things that Mike said last night. He says that Walter's ghost warned him that disasters would befall the country, including Herdwick district, now that the Bell could no longer be heard on the fells. He claims that Walter told him that it had already started with the recent election of a woman as Prime Minister and that things could only get worse. Here, I jotted them down to remember them. It's a long list.'

Selwyn consulted the clean inside of a split

Herdwick Breweries beermat on which he'd made notes.

'Walter predicted that England will never again win the World Cup, that there will be rioting in the streets over something called the Poll Tax, that the coal-mining industry will come to a violent end, that we'll fight a war over an island in the South Atlantic with Argentina – can you believe that? We're more likely to come up against Argentina in the final of the World Cup. He said that unemployment will reach record levels, manufacturing will disappear, interest rates and house prices will rocket upwards, Council-houses will be sold off, poverty and inequality will flourish and that there will be no such thing as Society any longer. His final prediction was that even if we revert to male Prime Ministers after that we will still have to endure many other hardships as a country ... foreign terrorist attacks, world-wide recession, climate-change, pandemics and something called Trump. It won't end until someone born within the sound of the Great Bell discovers an important new use for Herdwick wool to save the planet and change everything for the good again.'

'I agree, Mike sounds completely crazy. It all seems a bit far-fetched to me, Selwyn. Walter wasn't much of a feminist was he? I'm not surprised that his ghost doesn't approve of Maggie

Thatcher. Only time will tell if any of this is likely. I have my doubts. I mean, I've never heard of anything called Trump – does he mean a disease do you think?'

***

'So, Selwyn, Megan's coming home with the baby tomorrow?'

'As far as I know. I'll find out for sure when I go to the Maternity Unit later.'

'That's great. Then you're taking a week's holiday to help her out. I'm sure we can manage until you get back.'

Arthur and Selwyn were in Arthur's room at the Council Offices at the rear of Shepdale Town Hall. Selwyn had reported his conversation with Sheila to Arthur. Arthur asked,

'So, the other night. What did you make of Mike's or, rather, Walter's prediction?'

'Not much. England will win the World Cup again. They're bound to appoint Brian Clough as manager now, surely. What about Forest's European Cup Final Victory over Malmo in May? Absolutely brilliant.'

'No, not that. I mean the bit about *the country's bad luck running until someone born within the sound of the Great Bell discovers an important new use for Herdwick wool to save the planet and change everything for the good again.* It's hard to completely dismiss it as the ramblings of a madman when Mike had the exact wording of that missing verse.'

'Herdwick hasn't produced many world saviours over the centuries so far as I'm aware. We could be waiting a long time. Mike was nicknamed *Mad* for a reason. I've no idea what the prediction meant.'

'Well, you've got a new baby. Maybe Lisa will be that child.'

'I doubt it. Megan's already planning her future. It doesn't involve Herdwicks as far as I know unless she's thinking of teaching Lisa to knit bars of gold when she's older.'

'Fair comment. I just hope that we're both around to see that if and when it happens.'

'So do I.'

'So, will you be haunting the Tup for a pint tonight? It could be your last chance for a while.'

'I think that I could be persuaded. Perhaps we'll bump into Walter's ghost at closing time. We can ask him to fill us in on some more of the detail about his prediction.'

23: FOR THE GOOD OF THE FLOCK (1989)

Overnight the rivers of blood ceased to flow and the drain channels dried up. On the previous day the bleating of sheep, the squealing of pigs and the lowing of cattle had filled the air. The day after there was just an eerie silence. For thousands of years uninterrupted slaughtering had been carried out at that location, dating back to the days of the Neolithic pig-sticking pits soon to be investigated by archaeologists commissioned by Shepdale Museum. Now Shepdale Slaughterhouse had closed forever.

The men who worked there may have been regretting it but no-one else was. It had been a grim and unpleasant neighbour for the residents of the adjoining housing estate, especially when panic-stricken stock occasionally escaped and rampaged along the roads until the Police marksmen could end their terror. It was a nuisance to the shoppers, workers and tourists from the daily stream of stock wagons transporting the unfortunate victims to their fate, further clogging up the continually-busy main street through the town centre. Slaughtering had not ended in Herdwick district. It would continue at the modern, privately-owned Abattoir recently built near the new Motorway junction outside of town. It had just ceased to happen on the District Council-owned freehold within the town of Shepdale.

***

'The Clerk and Chief Executive called me in, Selwyn. He's got the Chairman of the Council on his back about the old Slaughterhouse site.'

Arthur, the Property Services Manager for Herdwick District Council, sat behind his desk in his office behind Shepdale Town Hall. Selwyn, his Estates Surveyor, sat opposite him. They were alone and the door was shut.

'What's Charles *beefing* about now?'

'Oh, very droll ... The Chairman has fired up the Liberals to support him on a job-creation scheme for the district. He wants the Slaughterhouse site to become a Business Park. Carve up the existing buildings into smaller units, build new starter units where the pens are and fill it all with new and expanding businesses. The Planners are on board and an application will be lodged soon. It will be voted through.'

'Fair enough. Anything's better than the existing use. So, what's the problem?'

'Well, the Council holds the freehold reversion. The Municipal Meat Company holds the lease from the Council. It's for 999 years at a nominal £1.00 per annum from sometime in the early 1960s.'

'Before my time. I've never needed to have any involvement with that Lease as it just runs and runs without rent reviews or breaks so there's never been any reason for me to look at it.'

'The Lease states that MMC "*shall not use the premises other than for the purposes of a public slaughterhouse.*" That's a very limiting restrictive covenant that prevents alternative uses without the Council's consent and because of that precise wording the Council doesn't have to be reasonable. It can unreasonably refuse consent if it wants to.'

'It sounds like we can demand a ransom payment from MMC in return for releasing them from the covenant so that they can redevelop the site as a Business Park.'

'In theory, yes. In practice, the Chairman wants Charles to arrange a free release in the interests of creating hundreds of jobs for the district.'

'I don't think that we can do that.'

'Neither do I, but we won't be popular if we say that. Can you have a think about it so we can talk again? Then I'll have to brief Charles.'

***

Blake Edwards was wealthy and bored. He'd made his money in property development in London and then retired to live in Winander. He had an enormous house with lake-frontage, a gin-palace moored out on the lake, a trophy second-wife and fingers in many business pies. Unable to settle for a life of ease, he'd run for the Council on a job-creation ticket a few years earlier and quickly risen to be the Leader of the Liberal Group, the largest party in the hung Council, and Chairman of the Council. He'd had the Clerk and Chief Executive's office relocated from its historic setting in Shepdale Town Hall into the three-storey Council offices at its rear and then commandeered the office next door to the Clerk and Chief Exec so that he could be on hand to control everything of importance that happened in the Council. Arthur and Selwyn felt that Charles Bowstead, the current Clerk and Chief Executive of Herdwick District Council was slowly being side-lined as Blake eased himself into an unhealthy position of power and influence. Charles, approaching retirement age, didn't seem able to prevent the shift.

***

'Arthur ... you and I are of a similar age. You must be thinking about retirement too, surely? I know that I am. Between you and me, it's a new world now and the likes of Blake Edwards rule the roost. Once over, the Chief Executive's position was respected. Our word was law. Now I'm regarded as little more than an adviser to the manager of a business. Edwards can't see that we have a wider duty to provide a service to the public that transcends basic commerce.'

Arthur and Selwyn were sat opposite Charles in his relocated office. Charles continued.

'We'll be able to get out of this trap soon, you and I. But you Selwyn ... you're going to have to adapt to new ways. Especially if you want to become Property Services Manager after Arthur. You're going to have to become a political animal on top of being a good manager.'

'It's not a prospect that I relish. But I'm only 41. I've no other choice as I need to get a higher salary and a load more years under my belt before I can think of retiring.'

'Anyway, what thoughts have you come up with in respect of this Slaughterhouse issue?'

Arthur leaned forward and lowered his voice a little.

'You know that the Council is bound by Section 123 of the Local Government Act 1972. That means that a local authority has the power to dispose of land but the main caveat to this power is that the Council must not do so for "*a consideration less than the best that can be reason-*

ably obtained".

"Land" is defined in section 270 of that Act as including *"any interest in land and any easement or right in, to or over land."*

Best consideration is generally interpreted as being the best price achievable in the open market. But it doesn't always have to be that if there are other relevant factors applicable. It's a subjective matter but the Bonner Report clarifies the Act by saying that best consideration should be assessed by one or more RICS or ISVA qualified valuers.

If I understand you correctly, Charles, the Chairman has consulted his own Solicitor and considers that S123 can be more generously interpreted.'

'Yes, firstly he thinks that the covenant does not constitute an interest in the land. Secondly he thinks that best consideration can be interpreted as a lot of new jobs created for the district by the new development instead of money. So he wants us to release the covenant without demanding a monetary ransom payment. As the Council's valuer are you prepared to certify that as best consideration, Selwyn?'

'No. I think that he's wrong on both points.'

'Arthur and I tend to agree with you. I've basically forgotten all my property law over the years that I've spent running the Council. But something just doesn't feel right. Call it gut instinct. What sort of monetary value would you put on the site if it was sold unrestricted?'

'The Council's freehold with the current lease in place is next-to-worthless to the Council. The Lease with the restrictive covenant limiting the use to a slaughterhouse is also virtually worthless to MMC now that the new slaughterhouse has been built. There isn't enough business for two slaughterhouses. But put the Freehold and the Lease together, with the covenant relaxed and planning consent for a Business Park, and they have a significant value. Each side needs the other. I reckon the two interests together are worth about half a million pounds in total. So the ransom for the release should be worth say 50% of that to the Council.'

'So, what can we do about it, Selwyn?'

'Two things. If you can stall the Chairman for a bit longer I propose to use Arthur's membership of the Local Authority Valuers' Association - LAVA for short - to see what help they can give me. They can trawl all their members in other authorities for opinions and examples of best practice. They include some pretty big County and Metro Councils which employ some very knowledgeable and experienced surveyors.

Some of them must have wrestled with this problem before. Also, the Chairman's interest in this matter may be genuine but, nevertheless, it wouldn't do any harm to check if he has any kind of a financial relationship with MMC that he hasn't declared. Something doesn't quite smell right. The Treasurer could use his Credit Agents to research that company and check his interests.'

'Let's do it. But keep it quiet and report directly back to me.'

Selwyn glanced at Arthur, signalling him to remain seated, and said,

'Just a suggestion Charles, but it might be useful if you could ask the Chairman to clarify his precise intentions in writing ... you know ... just so that we can understand exactly what it is that he wants. You could tell him that as his request is a little unusual that we don't want to mess it up for him. Also, you might even casually request a copy of his Solicitor's legal advice... just to make us feel more comfortable about agreeing with him.'

***

'We had the meeting with Blake last week. Sorry that I haven't been able to say anything sooner. I was waiting for it all to be tied up formally before I talked to you.'

Arthur had called Selwyn into his office and closed the door behind him. Selwyn sat opposite him at the desk.

'How did it go?' was Selwyn's first question.

'As well as could be expected, I'm pleased to say.'

Selwyn breathed a big sigh of relief and smiled, 'And how did he take it?'

'Not well, but that was to be expected too. I'd never seen that side of him before although I suspect that Charles has suffered it from time to time. Blake really is a nasty piece of work when he lets his guard down. There was a lot of swearing and name-calling initially. Then he kicked us out. Then he rang his Solicitor before calling us back in. We didn't involve you just in case things didn't go as we'd hoped. You never know when you might cross paths with him again. But Charles and I had nothing to lose in a power struggle.'

'So what exactly happened?

Arthur leaned forward and pushed a brown envelope across the desk towards Selwyn.

'First things first. This document is from the Personnel Section. All you have to do is sign both copies and leave one copy with me. Then they can start looking for someone to replace you.'

'Thanks, but I'll miss you ... and Charles too. So please tell me all about it.'

***

'Hello Charles ... and Arthur too. Your secretary didn't say what this meeting was about, Charles. So what's going on?'

Blake indicated that they should seat themselves around his conference table in his office next door to the Clerk and Chief Executive's office.

'Sorry Blake I don't want it to seem as if Arthur and I are ganging up on you. It's not intentional. I could have done this on my own but I also wanted Arthur to see the outcome of our joint efforts.'

'It must be important to drag you and Arthur away from your busy jobs, Charles.'

'Yes, it is.'

'As you know, Arthur and I don't have long to serve with this Council. We both intend taking retirement within the next six months. We need to talk about succession planning.'

'The Council will be sorry to lose you both. You've both been here for a long time. But everyone has to go sometime.'

'Yes, even you, Chairman.'

'What do you mean?'

'We've come to invite you to resign. Sometimes it's necessary to cull the faulty and the diseased for the good of the flock'

'WHAT!!!'

'Steady on, Blake. Try and control that rush of blood to the head. Just listen to what we have to say first.'

***

Megan had dropped Lisa off in the village with Ron, Selwyn's elder brother, and Mary, his wife. She and Selwyn were seated in a quiet corner of 'The Shepherd's Crook' pub where they'd first met. A pint and a half glass of Rampant Ram were placed on the table in front of them along with two menus.

'You've been very patient waiting for this explanation but the waiting is over. But just bear in mind that most of what I'm about to tell you is strictly confidential.'

Selwyn knew that he could trust Megan to keep it to herself but he still felt the need to say it.

'First of all, we're celebrating my promotion to Property Services Manager at Herdwick District

Council. Charles has arranged it so that the post does not have to be advertised. I'm the only internal candidate with a relevant RICS qualification. In any event they feel that I should be rewarded for my loyalty and professionalism. He will just report it as a decision made by him under his delegation in the urgent interests of service continuity. The Chair of the Personnel Sub-committee has agreed that it can go to the Sub-committee as a confidential report for noting only. I'll start the new job in three months' time when Arthur retires. It will mean more money and my own office.'

'Oh, well done you. That is good news. So, Arthur's retiring. Why is it confidential?'

'Well that bit isn't but the rest is.'

He outlined the background leading up to Blake's meeting with Charles and Arthur and then added,

'So, Blake Edwards was on the fiddle. I went to the Local Authority Valuers Association and got a couple of Barristers' opinions on relatively similar cases from two big London Boroughs. It was quite clear that the release of a restrictive covenant was an interest in land so was caught by 'best consideration' as a disposal. I also confirmed that creating jobs did not qualify as 'best consideration' under Section 123.

So Blake's legal advice and his intention to give away the covenant for nothing were completely down the chute. Even worse, the Treasurer's Credit Agents researched MMC and found that he'd bought a financial interest in that company some years before. He'd kept that conflict of interest very quiet … and that takes some doing in a small town like Shepdale. He'd covered his tracks in some shell companies. Basically it was one of those companies that had fronted the relocation to the new Abattoir site. He'll be doing alright out of that. But he also wanted to cash in on the development of the old site too by not paying the ransom to the Council.'

'But didn't you need evidence? Wasn't it just your word against his?'

'Well it might have been but he was so confident of success and so keen to convince us that he was right that he rather foolishly put his intentions in writing to Charles backed up with a copy of his Solicitor's erroneous advice. So, Charles and Arthur suggested that Blake could either resign his seat on the Council immediately or have his attempted fraud investigated by the Section 151 Officer and the District Auditor, reported to the Police and spread all over the front page of the Herdwick Gazette. In the end he opted to go quietly. The Council will get its ransom payment, but even then, it will still be worthwhile for Blake to develop the site as a Business Park so he won't lose out … and the district will still get its new jobs.'

'Well done. And congratulations on the promotion. I assume that Charles and Arthur fixed that after all the fireworks were over.'

'Yes. I rather think that with all the upheaval - losing the Chairman, the Clerk and Chief Executive and the Property Services Manager all within a very short time – that they wanted to ensure that after the cull they were leaving someone behind with similar values in at least one responsible position to carry on their work.'

'The future's looking rosy then?'

'I think so. I've got you, a better job and a new baby. Life is good.'

24: THE FOURTH MUSKETEER (1994)

The Wandering Tup on Sheepfold Lane in Shepdale was packed with drinkers although it was still only late morning. Outside it was a pleasant late-summer day and the street was busy with shoppers and tourists. Selwyn, the Property Manager of Herdwick District Council was sat with Jim, the Council's Senior Committee Clerk and Eric from the Finance Group in the front window booth looking across at Shepdale Town Hall. They had helped themselves to a share of the roast lamb and mint sandwiches, mutton rolls and salad from the buffet provided by Arthur's family and each had a pint of Rampant Ram in front of them on the booth table. Eric was leading the conversation.

'This is a bit early but I'm not complaining. It means that we don't need to buy lunch if we're stopping for a while.'

'It's strange, us sitting here, without Arthur. Even though it's been five years since he retired, I still miss him,' Selwyn offered, looking at Arthur's empty seat.

The others nodded in agreement.

'It's disappointing to think that he only had five years enjoyment of his pension after paying in for forty years,' reflected Jim. 'I think I'll want a few more years than that before I go.'

'Yes,' Selwyn replied, 'I'll want as many years out of it as I pay in when it's my turn. That seems only fair. So if I retire at say sixty after forty years' service I'll expect to live to be a hundred to get my contributions back.'

'It doesn't work like that I'm afraid,' said Eric. 'I know it sounds a bit sad but occasionally I examine the actuarial tables…'

The others laughed.

'… I can't help it, I'm an accountant. Besides I was orphaned when I qualified in my twenties. Both my parents died within a short time of each other. So I have a bit of a personal interest in checking on my life expectancy.'

'That must have been hard,' said Jim. 'Was that around the time that you joined the Council?'

'Yes. I've no relatives now and won't have unless I marry someone and that doesn't seem likely. However it meant that I didn't really need to work. The pension, when I eventually get it, will be a bonus. My father was an accountant too and he was a shrewd investor so they left me fairly well-off and with a mortgage-free house. That's why I don't push for promotion like you two. I wouldn't want to succeed my boss like you did with Arthur, Selwyn. I quite like working. I don't hate accountancy despite most people thinking that it's a boring subject, but I don't want all the management responsibility and stress that goes with promotion. I just like trundling along doing what I enjoy doing.'

'There's a lot to be said for that,' echoed Selwyn. 'Being a manager is not all that it's cracked up to be. Coincidentally, I may have solved one of my stress-inducing problems recently. I've appointed a new Assistant Estates Surveyor. You know that the last one was a bit of a disappointment to say the least. Well, his replacement will be joining us later and you're in for a pleasant surprise.'

'Sounds intriguing,' said Jim. 'Anyway, well-done with Arthur's eulogy today, Selwyn. It was good to see the Parish Church packed to send him off and your words were very fitting.'

'Thanks. It was the least that I could do for Arthur. But what were you saying Eric, about actuarial tables?'

'I was just going to say that Arthur's demise, sad though it is, is really, if you look at it clinically, Arthur's way of helping us out with our pensions. He'd be the first to acknowledge the financial soundness of what I'm saying.'

Eric lowered his voice and continued.

'I can't shout this out with his wife visiting everyone in the room to thank us for attending the funeral today. However, it's just a matter of maths. If everyone paid into the Northshire Pension Fund for forty years and we all lived to collect the pension for forty years afterwards then there wouldn't be enough funds available to cover the liabilities. The fund works on average life expectancies. A certain number of people have to die within a short time of retiring so that their pension stops early and those savings are re-applied to meet the needs of those that live longer in retirement. So Arthur - God rest his soul as he was such a good friend and I'm sorry that he's gone - is one of those helping to maintain the balance of the funds for us to eventually benefit, for example, if you want to live to be a hundred Selwyn.'

'Thanks for that Eric. I'm not sure that I'm comfortable with the knowledge but I'll accept your professional expertise on the subject. Really all I want to do is retire, live a long and healthy life and claw back every penny that I've paid in. That seems like a fair outcome to me.'

'Who knows what the future holds for any of us,' said Jim. 'At least we were here to see him off. I like to think he'll be sat in some heavenly equivalent of the Wandering Tup having a pint of Rampant Ram and swapping stories about Herdwick district with old Walter Winster.'

'And I hope that when I go, that either you, Jim, or you, Selwyn, will have some nice words to say about me, in the same way that you honoured Arthur today.'

'Don't worry Eric, you're still just a youngster. What are you – didn't we celebrate your fortieth in this very pub not that long ago? You're three years younger than me and an incredible six years younger than Selwyn. You'll outlive us both. We'll probably be the ones boosting your pension in the long run even though you won't actually – or should that be 'actuarially' – need it.

Groans from Eric and Selwyn.

***

The item in the Order of Service for Arthur Croxteth (1924-1994) had introduced Selwyn to those who might not have known him.

'I'm honoured that Arthur's family have asked me to say a few words this morning. They asked me to keep it light-hearted. A few words are not enough to describe a fine man and a good friend. Keeping it light-hearted is almost impossible.

If Arthur had known that I was doing this he'd have said:

'You can only do your best. No-one can expect more than that."

He often said that.'

Selwyn looked up from the lectern and scanned the congregation packed into Shepdale Parish Church. His mouth was dry so he reached for his glass of water before continuing.

'You've heard from others about Arthur's life. His prowess on the sports field as a youth, his academic abilities, his role as a young squadron leader flying Spitfires in World War Two, his long and happy marriage. I intend to talk about Arthur as a surveyor.'

For 23 years I probably spent more time with him than most other people. Much of that time was spent in the offices at Shepdale Municipal Borough Council and later at Herdwick District Council, although, as many of you will know, our visits to the Wandering Tup accounted for numerous lunchtimes spanning both of those authorities. Over that time we developed a friendship that I valued highly.

Before I took on today's responsibility I asked the others at work what they thought of him. That everyone liked him was a universal theme.

Some enjoyed his relaxed demeanour – Arthur being so chilled out that he'd fall asleep in the car when being driven to meetings. Others were grateful for the patience and kindness he'd shown when training them. His politeness and forbearance in dealing with difficult Councillors or members of the public that most of us would have blown a fuse at was a hallmark of his character. Always being the first in the office to buy the ice-creams when the summer heatwave finally arrived was fondly recalled. That he enjoyed a pint was mentioned occasionally.'

The congregation laughed at that last remark.

'However, the most common description that cropped up was '*professional*'.

"Arthur was a professional, a true professional."

But what is a true professional?

'*Professional*' is a curious word. We don't use it about most people. The modern dictionary definition is:

"Someone engaged in a specified activity as one's main paid occupation rather than as an amateur."

But that could be anyone in any specialist, paid employment. I think what people really meant was something deeper, far more personal than that.

To most people, acting like a professional means working and behaving in such a way that others think of them as competent, reliable and respectful. Professionals are a credit not only to themselves but also to others. That was Arthur; he was the ultimate professional, providing steady, reliable and astute advice on all property matters at times of great change within the Council. People knew that, when they listened to Arthur, they could rely on whatever he said. Certainly I did.

Arthur and I go back to 1966, the year that England won the World Cup. I was still taking my A-levels when I visited Shepdale Town Hall to report some damage to a Council building that I'd spotted whilst out walking on the fells. Arthur, or Mr Croxteth as I then called him, was the Borough Surveyor. He must have spotted something in me that perhaps no-one else would have noticed. It ended up with him offering me a job at the Council. What's more, he saw my notes on fell-walking and took me off to see his friend at the Herdwick Gazette to talk about getting them published. I've always been impressed that a man of such high office could take the time to notice me and take a chance on a mere schoolboy on such a brief acquaintance. It was because he knew people. He was a remarkable judge of character. One of his many stock phrases, ones that I have adopted for myself over the years, includes:

'Half the skill of this job is about reading people.'

Arthur lived by that adage and applied it in every situation. I well remember the first time that I had to put that skill to the test as a young surveyor. He'd sent me to resolve a dispute over repairs to the Ulverpool Bank Clock. His faith in my judgement based on what he perceived as my ability to read character was something that I will always appreciate. His words at the time …

'Selwyn you can only do your best. I think that you're right so I'll back you whether it works or not,'

… filled me with the confidence to take a measured risk to get the right result. I couldn't have done it without his encouragement and support.

Another notable moment was when we concluded the negotiations for the relocation of the Abattoir. That encouragement and support was offered time and time again as we worked together, right from taking me with him into the new Property Department in 1974 up to the time when he decided to retire and helped me to succeed him as Property Manager. I owe him so much.

As we were both surveyors, both local to the area and both committed to public service we had a common outlook. Although older and more experienced than I he never treated me as an inferior. He put up with my endless questions about procedure and practice with infinite patience whilst I was learning from him.

As our friendship developed I started to join him for lunch at the Wandering Tup. Jim and Eric followed on. We knew that within the Council we'd acquired the nick-name of the four musketeers. It amused Arthur that people saw us like that - as guardians of the Council's interests - because that's exactly how Arthur saw us himself. All professionals working together representing three of the four pillars of the Council – Property, Finance and Democracy – we just lacked Legal - all serving a common purpose.

It may sound odd to say this but some of my fondest memories of Arthur stem from the time that we spent together in the Town Hall Basement … not everyone's ideal work location. It's where we keep our estates records and the Council's property deeds. Just prior to Local Government Reorganisation we set up camp down there to sort the Deeds needing transfer to the new Northshire County functions and sift through the deeds being transferred in from the redundant municipal, urban and rural districts. Arthur had the knowledge and understanding of what was required. But he also had enthusiasm for what might have seemed a relatively boring job. That enthusiasm transmitted itself to me.

We were both quite sad when the task was over. It was deeply satisfying, working side by side, away from the distractions of other people and telephones, discovering the new properties that we would soon become responsible for.

People liked Arthur because Arthur liked people. He always took time to talk to them. An enormous number of people proved how popular he was by continuing to enquire after him when he retired. He seemed to know every farmer in Herdwick and they knew him. His local knowledge was very extensive. It wouldn't have surprised me if he'd also known every field that they owned and every individual sheep that belonged to them. One of his other sayings that I've adopted is:

'There's no substitute for local knowledge, especially when you're negotiating.'

Arthur had local knowledge in abundance because he knew everybody.

He was an excellent surveyor, a skilful negotiator and a highly effective deal-maker. However, as Manager, he didn't have much time to enjoy using those skills. It's a sad fact of local government life that professionals move into management and away from what they do best. But Arthur was an excellent manager too. We had no disasters that we couldn't control, the budgets were spent to target, properties were maintained and income and capital receipts grew steadily year on year to underpin the Council's finances. He was as professional at management as he was at surveying.

And as a leader, the staff liked and respected him, even when forced to make those difficult decisions about restructuring that impacted upon people's jobs and ultimately their lives. I never heard anyone blame Arthur for causing their problems but I did hear many thanking him for resolving them ... because everyone knew that he applied the same standards to himself that he expected of them. As he so often said to each of us,

"You can only do your best. No-one can expect more than that."

And that is where I now depart from my light-heartedness.'

Selwyn turned his head to speak directly to Arthur's coffin in front of the altar.

'Arthur, to me you were one of the greatest men that ever lived. Your influence on my life has been immense and valuable. It will take me a long time to recover from your loss. Thank you for everything.'

***

The Great Shepdale Bell on the Town Hall struck

one o'clock. Selwyn was watching the door of the pub. As an attractive young woman entered he went to greet her. He guided her to the bar, bought her a bottle of water and steered her via the buffet before bringing her over to the booth to join Jim and Eric.

'Jim, Eric, I want to introduce you to Farah. She's my new assistant and I expect great things of her. Farah, this is Jim, he's the Senior Committee Clerk for the Council and Eric is an accountant in the Finance Group. They are my two particular friends.'

'And his greatest allies in the battle against the Cardinals within the council. Plonk your bottle and food on the table Farah and please take that empty seat,' said Eric.

'The Cardinals?'

'It's nice to meet you. Don't take any notice of Eric's strange sense of humour,' said Jim. 'You'll get used to it. I'll translate for you in a minute.'

'Likewise,' said Eric. 'Have you just started today?'

'Yesterday actually, but Selwyn said that I should settle in first before trying to meet people in the Council offices. It's so hard to remember who everyone is and what they all do. But he said that it was important to meet you two as soon as possible.'

'It's always a bit strange at first but hopefully you'll come to like us. We don't bite. Wouldn't you rather have a proper drink?' Eric half rose from his seat as if to walk to the bar.

'Thanks very much, but no. I don't drink alcohol. I've nothing against it, and nothing against coming in pubs either as you can see. It's just a matter of my religion. I'm a Muslim.'

'Fair enough, although I think you'll find that the three of us rather like alcohol, especially at lunchtime. Where are you from?'

Selwyn provided more detail:

'Farah is from Shepdale so she knows the district well. Her father's a local businessman. She has an estate management degree from Lanchester University. She's single, likes fell-walking, has worked in estate agency in Lanchester for twelve months and realises that there's far more to surveying than just selling houses. So she thinks, quite correctly, that she has more chance of passing her RICS Assessment of Professional Competence in twelve months' time if she varies her experience. She has a wish to work in public service and is not daunted by the prospect of slaving away for peanuts in local government for the next forty years until the pension kicks in. Does that sum up your interview accurately?'

'Well not exactly but it covers some relevant points.'

They all laughed.

'She is also the most outstanding applicant that I have ever had the pleasure of interviewing. I think Arthur would be pleased with my choice.'

Has Selwyn told you why we're here today?' asked Jim

'Yes, you're honouring the life of your old friend, Arthur, Selwyn's former boss. A great man so I've been told.'

'That's right, a great man and a good friend. It's a pity that you never met him. The four of us spent a lot of lunchtimes in here together until he retired. You're now sitting in his place. We'd hoped that Selwyn's last assistant would be the one to fill the gap left by Arthur. Sadly, it didn't work out that way. Hopefully, you'll become our fourth musketeer.'

'Ah! I get the reference …the battle against the Cardinals within the council. All for one and one for all.'

'See - I told you she was outstanding,' said Selwyn.

25: SEEKING BURIED TREASURE (1998)

'As the Chairman of the Chartered Surveyors' Junior Organisation's Northshire Branch I'm very pleased to welcome to this training event our guest speaker Selwyn, my boss and Property Manager to Herdwick District Council. I'll hand over to him straight away.'

Farah, the Estates Surveyor to Herdwick District Council, was standing behind the Chairman's table facing the seated ranks of the North-West's Junior RICS membership. They were in the Meeting Room on the first floor of Shepdale Town Hall. The Great Shepdale Bell in the clock tower above them boomed seven times. Coffee and biscuits had been consumed. The October night was dark outside and the rain spattered against the windows but inside it was warm and welcoming.

Selwyn rose from his chair beside Farah, glanced at his notes and began his address.

'Hello everyone. Thank you for that welcome Farah and thanks to all of you for inviting me here to speak to you. There's a hand-out covering my talk to refer to as we go along. Please make yourselves comfortable and if you nod off at least you can read about it afterwards. My subject tonight will cover the "Rules of Negotiation". Negotiation is an important part of your work and hopefully I can pass on some helpful tips that you young surveyors might benefit from.

Now, this may be a strange start to my talk but I make no apology for it. 'Treasure Island' by Robert Louis Stevenson is my all-time favourite story. I first saw the Disney film when I was five years old at the cinema in Lanchester. During the film my Mother developed severe toothache and we had to leave early. I'd seen enough by then to be hooked for life and couldn't wait to buy the book. I still read it. Maybe I'm peculiar but once I'd immersed myself in a career as a property negotiator I just couldn't help noticing that the negotiation between Captain Smollett and Long John Silver was very much like a property deal.

All negotiations are different but usually they all benefit from following certain rules. It's wise to follow them if you want the negotiation to be successful. Not everyone does and not every negotiation is successful. So you should try to learn from the process. No-one is born with negotiating skills. You can read about the theory in textbooks but good negotiators are honed by experience. Until that time, you can benefit from Robert Louis Stevenson's delightful written account.

So let me set the scene.

The Hispaniola has sailed to Treasure Island following Captain Flint's map in search of buried treasure. Secretly, most of the crew are pirates under the leadership of the ship's cook, Long John Silver. When they reach Treasure Island the pirates plan to arm themselves and take over the ship and seize the treasure map. Before they can do so the others of the ship's company learn of the plan and trick the pirates into going ashore. Squire Trelawney, Dr.Livesey, Captain Smollett, Jim Hawkins (the cabin boy) and the few-remaining loyal crew then leave the ship, taking arms and supplies, and after a skirmish causing death on both sides, occupy an old stockade on the island where there is fresh water. Unbeknown to them Ben Gunn lives alone in a cave on the island having been marooned there by Flint. Silver knows that he has to make a deal with those in the stockade if he wants to secure the treasure map. Initially Smollett represents the ship's company.

So we're set up for a negotiation. The Pirates are prepared to kill for the map, the other side wants to live to find the treasure. A simple enough situation but the devil is in the detail. Long John Silver calls for negotiations.

Let's watch a short excerpt from the film; the first meeting. Farah, can you do the honours please?'

Farah pointed a remote control at the projector and a video flickered to life on the screen to the side of Selwyn. They all watched and listened to the excerpt in silence until Farah stopped it.

'Right,' said Selwyn, 'I haven't developed toothache yet so let's continue. You should all have a short extract of that conversation from the book in the hand-out.'

The junior surveyors shuffled their papers until they found it. Then Selwyn continued.

'There are 10 Rules of Negotiation.

Rule No.1: Prepare

Fail to prepare and prepare to fail. Co-ordinated negotiation is key, especially if part of a team. Then you all need to ensure that you're on the same page. If solo, then you need to be clear about your alternatives; what you can do if negotiation fails. In this case the team of Smollett, Trelawney and Livesey had previously agreed a fall-back position.

"But our best hope, it was decided, was to kill off the buccaneers until they either hauled down their flag or ran away with the Hispaniola. From nineteen they were already reduced to fifteen, two others were

wounded, and one, at least – the man shot beside the gun – severely wounded, if he were not dead. Every time we had a crack at them, we were to take it, saving our own lives, with the extremest care."

Rule No.2: Assess Bargaining Power

This comes in many forms and you may often have more of it than you think. It is crucial to knowing where your strengths and weaknesses lie. It is not just something obvious, like market power, but can be subtler, such as relationship power or time deadlines.

Before the negotiation starts Trelawney, Livesey and Smollett are aware of a potential deadline that Silver is up against:

"And, besides that, we had two allies – rum and the climate.

As for the first, though we were about half a mile away, we could hear them roaring and singing late into the night; and as for the second, the doctor staked his wig that, camped where they were in the marsh and unprovided with remedies, the half of them would be on their backs before a week."

Rule No.3: Set the Scene

Surroundings and climate make a difference to negotiation. Choose the location carefully as it can reflect how the negotiation will play out. Cold and informal locations may inspire hostility, whilst a more informal setting may encourage warmth and agreement. In this case both men know that Smollett will not leave the safety of the stockade. Silver has to go to him. That suits Smollett as it assists him with two elements of the negotiation. Silver has to trust his safety under the flag of truce to Smollett and Smollett wants Silver where he can goad him as much as possible. So Smollett has all the advantages of location. As Silver says,

"We're willing to submit if we can come to terms and no bones about it. All I ask is your word, Cap'n Smollett, to let me safe and sound out of this here stockade, and one minute to get out o'shot before a gun is fired."

Rule No.4: Set the tone

From the start you should set out the terms of engagement. Everyone should agree to have a productive and respectful negotiation. It helps with clarity but also allows you to anchor back if anyone deviates from the point or wants to play tough.

Smollett again uses his advantage:

"My man, I have not the slightest desire to talk to you. If you wish to talk to me, you can come, that's all."

He also sets the tone by forcing Silver to climb

the stockade fence (Silver has only one leg) and walk uphill over tree stumps through soft sand with his crutch. When he arrives Smollett refuses to let him into the hut out of the cold. He also insults him,

"Why Silver, if you had pleased to be an honest man, you might be sitting in your galley. It's your own doing. You're either my ship's cook – and then you were treated handsome – or Cap'n Silver, a common mutineer and pirate, and then you can go hang!"

When Silver initially starts to make threats against Abe Gray, Smollett anchors him back:

"'If Abe Gray —'Silver broke out.

'Avast there!' cried Mr. Smollett. 'Gray told me nothing, and I asked him nothing; and what's more, I would see you and him and this whole island blown clean out of the water into blazes first. So there's my mind for you, my man, on that.'

This little whiff of temper seemed to cool Silver down. He had been growing nettled before, but now he pulled himself together."

This negotiation has not started well and, eventually, when Silver leaves no-one will help him to his feet, again in line with the hostile tone.

Rule No.5: Listen

Successful negotiation requires true understanding of the other party's wants, needs and motivations. This can only be achieved by listening and drawing out information from what they tell you. A good rule of thumb is to spend 2/3rds listening and only 1/3 speaking. Smollett has this off to perfection.

"If you have anything to say, my man, better say it."

Silver cannot resist praising Smollett for something that happened during the night.

"Well, now, you look here, that was a good lay of yours last night ... Some of you pretty handy with a handspike-end. ... He wasn't dead when I got round to him, not he."

Smollett knows nothing about this but by saying very little and listening he learns something to his advantage; that another pirate has been killed (by Ben Gunn) and that the odds in battle have just improved in the company's favour.

Then they sit smoking in silence until Silver, again, cannot resist breaking the silence and is forced to make the opening bid in the negotiation. We'll examine that later.

Rule No.6: Enjoy it

Negotiation can be tense, drawn out and stressful. Learn how to turn it into an enjoyable experience and everyone will be thankful. In particular, avoid emotion.

It's clear that Silver at least does not enjoy it and cannot keep a lid on his emotions. Stung by Smollett's comments he becomes unpleasant and threatening:

'Then he spat into the ground.

"There!" he cried. "That's what I think of ye. Before an hour's out, I'll stove in your old block house like a rum puncheon. Laugh, by thunder, laugh! Before an hour's out, ye'll laugh upon the other side. Them that die'll be the lucky ones."

And with a dreadful oath he stumbled off.'

Such threats and oaths were hardly likely to work on a man like Smollett, an ex-navy captain and used to being obeyed, a man who could keep his emotions under control even in the most stressful of situations. Contrast this reaction:

'Captain Smollett rose from his seat and knocked out the ashes of his pipe in the palm of his left hand.

"Is that all?" he asked.'

with

'Silver's face was a picture; his eyes started in his head with wrath. He shook the fire out of his pipe.'

Smollett is enjoying the exchange, Silver is not.

Rule No.7: Hard men don't win.

Successful negotiation should create a deal that both parties feel good about. Win-win, not all out to win. Negotiating fairly and with respect will enhance your reputation as a negotiator. In this case two hard men show no intention of reaching agreement. Smollett is stubborn and Silver is arrogant. Smollett admits later that he has goaded Silver on purpose, reasoning that battle is probably inevitable and might as well be fought sooner as later while they are alert and fresh.

"I've given Silver a broad-side. I pitched it in red-hot on purpose; and before the hour's out …we shall be boarded."

Clearly that's no way to reach agreement. As a result Silver storms off in a rage and Smollett is left to organise the defence of the stockade.

Rule No.8: Know when to quit.

Sometimes negotiations hit a brick wall. Then it might pay to break and regroup, or to be open and discuss the impasse frankly. If that doesn't work then perhaps the deal cannot be done. Some deals are just not meant to be, new information may come to light, which changes the whole equation.

If we look at the opening offer from Silver:

"You give us the chart to get the treasure by, and drop

shooting poor seamen and stoving of their heads in while asleep. You do that, and we'll offer you a choice. Either you come aboard along of us, once the treasure's shipped, and then I'll give you my affy-davy, upon my word of honour, to clap you somewhere safe ashore. Or if that ain't to your fancy, some of my hands being rough and having old scores on account of hazing, then you can stay here, you can. We'll divide stores with you, man for man; and I'll give my affy-davy, as before to speak the first ship I sight, and send 'em here to pick you up."

...and then the counter offer from Smollett:

"If you'll come up one by one, unarmed, I'll engage to clap you all in irons and take you home to a fair trial in England. If you won't, my name is Alexander Smollett, I've flown my sovereign's colours, and I'll see you all to Davy Jones. You can't find the treasure. You can't sail the ship — there's not a man among you fit to sail the ship. You can't fight us — Gray, there, got away from five of you. Your ship's in irons, Master Silver; you're on a lee shore, and so you'll find. I stand here and tell you so; and they're the last good words you'll get from me, for in the name of heaven, I'll put a bullet in your back when next I meet you. Tramp, my lad. Bundle out of this, please, hand over hand, and double quick."

It's pretty clear that negotiations have hit a brick wall. As I said earlier, Smollett is prepared to walk away – he can risk deliberately provoking Silver. So they break and Silver mounts his onslaught against the stockade to try and change the situation.

We can't watch an excerpt from the film because Disney's screenplay is a re-write and they changed the story. So you need to refer to the second extract in your hand-out.'

The junior surveyors shuffled their papers again and Selwyn continued.

'Livesey then acquires new information on which to promote the second negotiation meeting. Both he and Silver have already learnt that the Pirates are not strong enough to take the stockade by force, following the failure of their attack. Then Livesey learns that the map is worthless. A follow-up meeting producing a new deal – the map in return for safe relocation – shows Livesey and Silver reacting to new information following the failure of that initial meeting.

Rule No.9: Offer Loose Change.

This is something that has value to the other party but not so much to you. Discovering the other party's motivation can allow you to keep the loose change for later in the negotiation. A classic example is the salesman throwing in an extended guarantee with a used car to clinch a deal. He gets his price at an insignificant cost to him but you get valuable peace of mind if anything goes wrong.

This goes hand in hand with the suggestion that you should never offer something in a negotiation without getting something back.

Loose change never comes into the initial meeting between Smollett and Silver as they are so far apart on fundamentals. However, when Smollett is shot, Livesey takes over for the second meeting. Livesey changes the venue – going out to find Silver – and changes the tone to create trust.

"Well," says the doctor, "Let's bargain."

This time Livesey is aware that Ben Gunn has moved the treasure to his cave on the two-pointed hill so the map is worthless. He also knows that the ship has disappeared. So Livesey is able to make a deal. There is an exchange of loose change. The map (very valuable to the Pirates) in exchange for the chance to relocate from the stockade (very valuable to the Company) but neither worth anything to the other side:

'... he had gone to Silver, given him the chart, which was now useless – given him the stores, for Ben Gunn's cave was well-supplied with goat's meat well salted by himself - given anything and everything to get a chance of moving in safety from the stockade to the two-pointed hill, there to be clear of malaria and

to keep a guard upon the money.'

Rule No.10: Remember Win-Win

My biggest tip is to remind you of Rule No 7. Hard men don't win. Negotiating is about getting a good deal; not destroying the other party. You may have to meet again when the boot is on the other foot. Livesey and Silver think that they have achieved a good deal after the second meeting.

We discussed Smollett and Silver earlier – both hard men. On 10th of April this year, some hard men concluded a very complex and bitter negotiation. I refer, of course, to the Good Friday Agreement for peace in Northern Ireland. None come any harder than the main antagonists, Martin McGuinness and Ian Paisley. Both sides won, neither side lost. No-one was crushed. Whilst neither was ecstatically happy, they both walked away with a successful deal acceptable to each side. That's how it should be. Many said it would never happen. And neither side has been stupid enough to brag about their successes because that deal had to be based on trust. Lives still depend upon it.

Now, let's talk about what you've seen and heard and I'll try to answer any questions.

Let me pose the first one. Who thinks that the company should have remained aboard the

Hispaniola to strengthen Smollett's negotiating position? Would that have been a better choice of location?'

***

Eventually, Selwyn drew the discussion to a close.

'And finally, the buried treasure you've all really come for. A Continuing Professional Development Certificate for each of you to prove to the Royal Institution of Chartered Surveyors that you've attended this event and can tick another two hours off your compulsory annual training requirement.'

26. F & M (2000)

The fires burned day and night. The smoke hung over the countryside like a grey army blanket, cloaking the weak sun on fine days or blending into the miserable rain on others. At night the sky turned a dirty, streaked pink from the continual glow of piled carcasses being incinerated. Trapped in the void between the land and the smoke, the smell of burning meat hovered over everything as a constant reminder of death.

Country roads were filled with trucks, belching out diesel fumes to add to the smog, delivering the condemned and collecting the despatched, splashing through disinfectant checkpoints as they hauled their grisly cargo from the farms to the burial sites. Everywhere were vets, soldiers, slaughter-men engaged in an efficient, endless killing-exercise. And everywhere there were innocent victims caught up in it. It was a war unlike any other war; eerily-quiet; without the noise of battle. And striding amongst the carcasses was a military figure, sometimes sucking on a cigarette, sometimes making notes on the back of a cigarette packet, sometimes wondering what the hell he'd taken on and all the time applying bloody-minded determination and offering leadership.

***

It had started for Selwyn, the Property Manager for Herdwick District Council, in February 2000 when the Chief Exec had called him to his office in the modern extension at the back of Shepdale Town Hall.

'We have a big problem, Selwyn. That serious foot and mouth outbreak from the north of the county has started to spread south. If it gets a hold down here it could mean the end for Herdwick sheep and the district of Herdwick as we know it. The Government is throwing a lot of resources at it. They've called in the army and there's a Brigadier in charge. He wants to set up a local control centre somewhere around Shepdale. Can we help?'

'What does he need? An empty building, lots of rooms for offices and storage of cleaning equipment, a mess room and kitchen, toilets, car parking?'

'Yes, that's the kind of thing. They'll bring their own equipment and telephones and furniture. We can charge them a rent plus running costs but, between you and me, don't take advantage of the situation. Keep it fair. In fact, see if you can find a way to make it rent free. It's in the district's interests not to hinder them. I know what you're like about getting blood out of a stone.'

'That's not a problem. If it's a short term letting for less than seven years then the Council isn't obliged to charge a market rent. Let me talk to Farah. We have a property that should meet their needs. I take it that you're prepared to use your emergency delegation powers if need be?'

***

Back in the office Selwyn immediately sought out Farah.

'Farah, let me ask you something please. You're handling that dilapidations claim against Northshire County Council regarding the old Stonecleft building that County Social Services rents from us as an old people's home. How's it going?'

'We've just agreed a cash settlement. Their notice to quit on the lease expired some months ago. They've relocated all the residents to modern premises with en-suite facilities as you know. My report's gone to the Property Committee to recommend sale as we've no use for it. It'll go on the market as soon as the principle of disposal is approved. Why do you ask?'

'You might have to stall your report. It could be that we have a temporary use for it. Sorry to mess up your plans but can you ring this Brigadier bloke and get him out there to have a look at it pretty quickly please? You can handle the negotiations as it's your case but I'd like to come with you to meet him, just out of interest. I've been reading about him in the papers. The Chief Exec's involved. It's top priority.'

***

The Cistercian monks of Ulverpool Abbey first farmed the local fells. The Herdwick breed may have already been part of their flocks. However it seemed more likely that those calm, unemotional animals with sad, white faces and scruffy fleeces and the *"blessing of greeting frae yon li'l grey sheep"* so lauded in the works of Walter Winster, the internationally-renowned Herdwick dialect poet, were probably brought over by Norse settlers in the 10th century. Nobody really knew but what was certain was that they had been native to the area for a thousand years. Now their existence was under threat from mass culling, possibly to the point of extinction.

Selwyn knew all about those sheep. He'd encountered them all his life. He'd seen them from childhood, travelling through Shepdale on their way to and from the auction mart, on the hills when he'd been out recording and sketching for his fell-walking books and later on the land that he let for grazing on behalf of the Council. He could still remember some of Winster's verse drummed into him at junior school.

"Oot on't fells and doon in't valleys,
Us weary 'eart ferly rallies
From t'sound o't bleating
Whene'er us meeting
That most bless_ed_ of greeting
Frae yon li'l grey sheep."

Selwyn's older brother, Ron, ran some Herdwicks on the crag at the rear of his farm although Ron diversified into milk and beef cattle to spread his risk. Herdwicks were an important part of the local farming and tourist industries but Ron had told Selwyn that it didn't do to depend upon them solely for an income. Farming could be a precarious living at the best of times. That was clearly being proved as the Brigadier's plans were being put into practice.

***

As spring and summer wore on Selwyn stayed away from the fells. Like the rest of the population he was prevented by the closure orders. Not since the great heatwave of 1976 had the uplands been so empty of fell-walkers. The scourge of foot and mouth disease had spread through the Herdwick district fell country, potentially bringing financial disaster with it. It had to be checked quickly to prevent the disease not only ruining the background to a million snapshots but shattering a long-established way of country life and wrecking the tourist industry.

The Council's Leisure Services Manager told Selwyn,

'The fell farmers and their Herdwicks have created this landscape. If the sheep are slaughtered and the fells cleared, everything will change. Rough scrubland and coarse grasses will quickly take over the landscape. Moss, bogs and marshes will proliferate. Gorse and juniper will spread. Those close-cropped upland pastures will disappear. There'll be nobody to look after those crumbling dry-stone walls. The whole landscape will decline. Only about five per cent of the people who come to this district don't come to walk. Walking is the whole point. People won't come here if they can't. The tourism industry across Northshire County is worth £964 million and most of it's centred on this district.'

'Surely the farmers will bounce back and then the tourists will return?'

'It's unlikely. I've heard that tens of thousands of sheep are being killed every week, Breeders think that Herdwicks might disappear from the county altogether, and with them the genes of an entire ancient breed. Whilst not rare at the moment, because there are an estimated 60,000 Herdwicks, you have to remember that ninety-five per cent of them are found in Northshire alone. They're seriously at risk of extinction."

Herdwicks were a special breed that freely roamed the fells, seeking out the best grass. Their coarse, water-resistant wool enabled them to live up on the rain-soaked fell tops in all weathers. They were only brought down to the enclosed fields near to the farms for very short periods for lambing, dipping and shearing. Without fences on the fells the sheep passed freely from one farmer's grazing area to the next. Their most remarkable feature was their homing instinct. They stuck to their own part of the high ground and the ewes taught their lambs to always graze that same area. When taken away for lambing they instinctively returned there. That homing instinct, if destroyed by mass slaughter, could never be restored.

Selwyn thought back to his and Farah's meeting with the Brigadier. They'd wandered through the rooms in the old Stonecleft building. It was a rambling, detached, slate-built two-storey structure with a pitched roof. It comprised a central block with a wing at each end. Looking over the main road into Shepdale at the very edge of town, within its own grounds and surrounded by a wall enclosing tarmac areas for parking, it offered an ideal location for the control centre for the south of the county. Plenty of rooms for admin and storage, together with kitchens and toilets, made it ideal for organising, accommodating, feeding and watering the small army of vets and soldiers that might need to report there before fanning out across the surrounding countryside to help stop the spread of the disease. Its relatively isolated location meant that the neighbours would not be upset by any noise and the disinfecting of vehicles, equipment and footwear could be contained within the site. Its only drawback was the all-invading stench of urine that had soaked into its very fabric from decades of elderly residents.

The Brigadier had already become the darling of the press. It was easy to see why. Tall, well-built and immaculately-turned out even in his camouflage denims and black boots, he oozed confidence. Personally brought in by the Prime Minister to help resolve the problem, he was organising and managing the logistics to clear the backlog of 150,000 carcasses piling up on farms across the county. He had an imposing presence.

As Farah talked terms Selwyn studied the craggy features beneath the beret on the Brigadier's large square head; the bayonet gaze of his blue eyes, the bent bridge of his battered nose, the firm set of his mouth over the central cleft of his solid, square jaw. This was a man at the height of his powers, experienced, assured and in total control. He'd read about the Brigadier in the Herdwick Gazette – a man with a plan as they'd described him. When the foot and mouth crisis was seemingly out of control the Brigadier had stepped forward, postponed his retirement and offered his services. The papers had seized on one particular quote of his:

'Then I realised that it was very simple. You had two lots of kit, one live and one dead, and you had to pick them up and dump them somewhere else. The basic plan I drew on the back of a cigarette packet on the bonnet of my car.'

'Sorry about the smell from the carpets,' said Farah.

'Not to worry,' laughed the Brigadier. 'We're used to rough conditions. Have you ever been close up to the rear end of a Herdwick? That's not too pleasant either.'

Selwyn smiled. He knew exactly what the Brigadier meant. As a sixth-former he'd spent his summers unloading fleeces at his holiday job in the Herdwick Farmers' Cooperative warehouse in Shepdale. Any-one who inadvertently got on the wrong side of the foreman could easily find themselves assigned to re-stack the dag pile on a hot summer's afternoon; dags being the soiled wool clippings from around the blunt end of a sheep, sweating in plastic 'proven' bags until there were enough to fill a wagon for transporting to Bradford for washing. And giving off a smell that, once experienced, was not easily forgotten.

Farah was winding up the negotiation.

'So we're agreed, Brigadier. It has to be a fixed term tenancy of less than seven years to avoid the Council's legal requirement to obtain a best consideration rent under Section 123 of the Local Government Act 1972. It can't be a running six-monthly tenancy for example. So you'll take a six months fixed-term tenancy of the entire building and grounds. No rights to extend or renew beyond that, although if you need it and if you ask I'm confident that the Council will see its way to accommodating such a request but we just can't put it in writing at this stage. You'll pay a peppercorn rent, meet all running costs and outgoings, be responsible for all day-to-day running repairs and hand back the premises in no worse a condition than at the start of the tenancy as evidenced by an ingoing, photographic schedule of condition.'

'That's fine. Can you e-mail those terms to me as a formal offer with your Solicitor's contact details please? I'll also need a copy of the photographic schedule.'

'No problem. Technically you should obtain planning consent but there's no time for that in the current crisis. So the Chief Executive of the Council will stick his neck out and use his emergency delegation to ensure that the Planners understand the situation. The Councillors will applaud him for helping you. When do you want to occupy?'

'Tomorrow if that's possible.'

'Ok. Take this set of keys and start making your arrangements. I'll wander around, take photos for the record of condition and pull the door shut on my way out. It's all yours as from now.'

'Thank you Farah. I wish all my problems were as easy to resolve.'

***

By September the crisis was over. The Brigadier had sent the keys back and Farah dusted off her report recommending the sale of the building.

'Well done.'

The Chief Exec had called Selwyn and Farah into his office to congratulate them.

'We only played a small part and it was a team effort,' said Selwyn.

'Nevertheless you came up with a good solution and you applied it quickly and sensibly. The Councillors were happy with the outcome. Herdwick district has been very lucky indeed. We only lost one tourist season and with a bit of luck those farmers who were affected will survive with the help of Government compensation. It looks like we came out of it better than the northern half of the county. In the end, the Herdwick breed as a whole didn't need saving. Foot and Mouth Disease never established itself on the highest of the fells where only the Herdwicks can go. Around 20,000 were culled, but many escaped the cull, saved by the very qualities that have sustained them through the centuries – the ability to live where no other breed of sheep can survive.'

'Farah and I were just glad to be able to help.'

'Well this is local government, Selwyn. I can't imagine that you expected any other reward than the satisfaction of knowing that you served your community well... once again.' Then the Chief Exec laughed at his own joke.

'Certainly not,' said Selwyn, shaking his head.

'By the way, there's no rest for the wicked. I've got another task for the pair of you. As a result of that scare, that the Herdwicks could have been wiped out completely and with it the district's economy, I've been approached by a local geneticist. He's accessed Government DEFRA grants and NFU backing with support from the Tourist Board to set up the Herdwick Trust. He's looking for some modern, local industrial premises to establish a small genetic research and storage facility for samples of sperm and embryos taken from Herdwicks to protect them against total wipe-out in the future. He wants to examine just what makes them tick. Apparently, even though they're as tough as old boots we can't just rely on the Herdwicks to save themselves again. It's too worrying, so the Councillors want to invest in the Trust and its sperm bank for the future.

I thought that you might have a spare nursery unit to let in one of those starter estates that the Council set up in partnership with the Rural Development Agency in the 1990s to create local employment. It sounds an ideal use for that sort of thing. Here's his contact details.'

'We'll get straight on it …'

As they closed the door Selwyn whispered to Farah.

'… after lunch, that is. Since there's no other reward do you fancy a mutton pie and a drink, on me, in the Wandering Tup? Jim and Eric will be there. They'll want to know what the Chief Exec just said to us.'

'Might as well, thanks.'

They walked in silence through the offices towards the corridor that linked them to the Town Hall until Farah observed,

'It's a strange world that we work in. We've just been thanked for assisting with an exercise to kill most of the district's sheep. Now we're being asked to help with an exercise to preserve their blood-line for the future.'

'That's always the way with property,' said Selwyn. 'No matter what the Council does it always involves either occupying property, making money from it or managing it on behalf of the community. It's what keeps us in a job.'

NOTE FROM THE AUTHOR

"The art of writing requires a constant plunging back into the shadow of the past where time hovers ghost-like." – Ralph Waldo Ellison, American Novelist.

If you find this to be a disappointing place to leave these stories then please be aware that if you return to the start of this book to 'The Final Vote' you can just continue reading on from where the last story ends ... in a sort of perpetual time-loop.

ACKNOWLEDGEMENT

ACES

Herdwick Tales began life as 'The Selwyn Series'; short stories published quarterly by the Association of Chief Estates Surveyors and Property Managers in Local Government (ACES), exclusively for its membership, in its professional magazine the 'ACES Terrier'. Now all 26 stories have been gathered together in this one volume to be enjoyed by a wider audience.

The author wishes to acknowledge the suport and encouragement offered by Tim Foster and Betty Albon, successive editors of the 'ACES Terrier'.

The author also wishes to thank former ACES member Martin Haworth for contributing suggestions to help improve the series.

ABOUT THE AUTHOR

David Lewis Pogson

David Lewis Pogson was born and still lives in Northern England. For 50 years he practiced as a surveyor becoming a Fellow of the Royal Institution of Chartered Surveyors. His career required him to write endlessly ... reports, letters, particulars, bids ... which earned him a living but gave him little creative satisfaction. He realised that he needed to 'scratch the creative itch' and so, around the age of 50 years, he started to write articles on surveying topics and work experiences for a professional magazine which allowed him to introduce some controversy, humour and the odd bit of fiction. He was paid a backhanded compliment by one reader who said "You have the ability to turn a totally bor-

ing subject into something half-way readable."
Buoyed by this success he branched out into short stories and poetry and has been published in a variety of media. Along the way he won:

 - The Cumbria Local History Federation Prize for his paper on 'The Ulverston Bank Clock' which he published as a book.

 - The Freerange Theatre Company's Playframe Short Story competition for 'Affordable Principles' which the Company converted into the play 'Tin Can Lurky' which then toured rural venues and

 - Several Microcosmsfic Flash Fiction Competitions.

Read more from him at: www.davidlewispogson.wordpress.com
or google him using
amazon+ david lewis pogson
or see his short videos on
youtube+davidlewispogson

Printed in Great Britain
by Amazon